Romance On Four Worlds

Betts Branch
4862 South Salina Street
Syracuse, NY 13205

Romance On Four Worlds:
A Casanova Quartet
by Tom Purdom

"Romance in Lunar G" first published in *Asimov's Science Fiction*, November 1995. Copyright 1995 by Tom Purdom.

"Romance in Extended Time" first published in *Asimov's Science Fiction*, March 2000. Copyright 2000 by Tom Purdom.

"Romance with Phobic Variations" first published in *Asimov's Science Fiction*, February 2001 Copyright 2001 by Tom Purdom.

"Romance for Augmented Trio" first published in *Asimov's Science Fiction*, February 2004. Copyright 2004 by Tom Purdom.

Collection © 2015

This is a work of fiction. All the characters and events portrayed in this book are either fictitious or are used fictitiously.

All rights reserved. Printed in the United States of America. No part of this book may be used or reproduced in any manner without written permission except for brief quotations for review purposes only.

In-house editor: Darrell Schweitzer

Fantastic Books
1380 East 17 Street, Suite 2233
Brooklyn, New York 11230
www.FantasticBooks.biz

First Edition ISBN 10: 1-62755-635-4
First Edition ISBN 13: 978-1-62755-635-4

First Edition

Though pedantry denies,
'Tis plain the Bible means.
That Solomon grew wise
While talking with his queens.
—William Butler Yeats

Table of Contents

Romance in Lunar G. 9
Romance in Extended Time. 40
Romance with Phobic Variations. 80
Romance for Augmented Trio. 111
Afterword: Giacomo Casanova. 147

ROMANCE IN LUNAR G

I was alone, well outfitted, well supplied with jewels,
without letters of recommendation, but with four hundred
zecchini in my purse, a complete stranger in the great
and beautiful city of Milan, in excellent health, and at the
happy age of twenty-three. It was January in the year 1748.
　—Giacomo Casanova, *History of My Life*, tr. Willard R. Trask

I was almost sixty when I finally read Casanova's memoirs. People had been telling me I should read Casanova ever since I had reached my late twenties, but I probably wouldn't have read him when I was fifty-eight if my finances had been in shape. I had been caught in the whirlwind that raced through the currency markets in 2054. It took me six months to get back to where I could face a restaurant bill without cringing.

It wasn't hard to understand why readers who were familiar with the memoirs thought I would find them interesting. I had always assumed Casanova was a mere compulsive—a man who was trying to run up a score. Instead, I discovered the pages of his autobiography are crowded with statements I could have written myself. If three competent behavioral physiologists read a random sample taken from all twelve volumes, at least two of them would be absolutely convinced he and I could be described with the same parameters.

There was, of course, a significant difference in our circumstances. Casanova never knew that his responses to women could be traced to a few thousand cells in two precisely mapped areas of his brain. He didn't have to live with the knowledge he could slip into a modification clinic and permanently dampen the emotions that dominated his life. In his world, character was destiny—not personal choice.

"You're supposed to be watching the scenery," Shezuko said.

We were standing on the observation deck, watching the sunrise as it tapped the upper reaches of the lunar mountains in front of us, and Shezuko had noticed the look on my face when Malita Divora and Wen Kang had stepped out of the elevator. The big cruise vehicle was crawling along the dark side of the terminator, in the exact spot the sales spiels had promised it would occupy at this moment. One hundred and forty-eight people had arranged themselves in front of the oval viewing windows that faced the sunrise. One hundred and forty-seven were staring at the gleaming, rounded summits that floated over a landscape illuminated by dim blue Earthlight.

Shezuko was smiling, but she wasn't laughing at me. Of all the women who've befriended me, I think she understood me the best.

It was one of the blacker moments in one of the blacker periods of my life. At dinner the night before, Malita had chosen a table next to ours and systematically flaunted her relationship with Wen. Every time I had glanced their way, Malita had been looking at Wen as if she wanted to record every word he was saying. I had managed to keep up a conversation with Shezuko but I can still remember most of the things they talked about. Over the salad, Wen told her anecdotes about one of his mother's more famous conquests. Over the rice and rabbit, with apple and mushroom sauce (I remember every detail!), Wen compared the two sports that had given him his biggest taste of celebrity and Malita chatted about the discontents of the children she had interviewed for a piece on long-term marriage arrangements. Over dessert (an outlandish helping of fruit and whipped cream which Wen consumed with outlandish enthusiasm), she led Wen into a little shop talk and they dissected the pros and cons of the one subject that seems to fascinate journalists and most of the other people who work with the databanks: the benefits of pay-per-view versus flat-rate listings.

I have always avoided the embarrassments of jealousy. It is a childish emotion that has nothing to do with the passions I have spent my life cultivating. In this case, I even knew they had both opted for major reductions in their sex drives, so they could concentrate on "aspects of life we find more satisfying." They had actually gone to the extra expense of renting separate cabins. I was dealing, however, with an intelligent, creative woman who had decided to evict me from her life. When they had left the table, it had been obvious Wen was going to join Malita in her quarters.

Now, fifteen hours after I had last seen her, Malita paused two steps from the elevator and tipped back her head when she saw me looking at her. Wen Kang rested his hand on her shoulder and soaked in the atmosphere with the honest pleasure of someone who loved the human glitter in the foreground as much as he loved the panorama outside. Lunar society was going through one of those periods when men wear their hair long and women crop it close—a fashion that emphasized Wen's fleshy sensuality and Malita's alert, restless intelligence.

"I still find it difficult to believe you feel the rewards outweigh the disadvantages," Shezuko said. "I would think that for someone who loves pleasure as much as you do…"

"Is it any different for you?" I said. "Are your feelings any different from mine when you reach the end of an encounter?"

"But I know I'm going to enjoy myself first. For you, there's no guarantee you'll enjoy anything."

If you've ever spent any time with Shezuko Okada's work, you know sexual love is as important to her as it is to me. The aesthetic and emotional impact of her fantasies rests on a single poignancy: the fact that the most intense and devoted bondings must inevitably yield to time. In the middle of her sixth decade, she had made a very sensible decision and opted for a personality modification that eliminated the kind of unpleasantness I was experiencing. Her passions didn't burst into flame until she knew they were based on a mutual attraction. Her involvements were just as intense as mine—and most of them didn't last any longer—but Shezuko knew they would traverse a predictable arc.

Wen and Malita joined a foursome that included a genetic engineer who had been living on the Moon since the first laboratory complex had been carved into the rim of Eratosthenes crater. Every time I sneaked a glance in their direction—which was about once every minute—Malita was responding to the engineer's pronouncements with the animation that characterized everything she did. She was one of those conversationalists who look just as sprightly when they're listening as they do when they're talking.

It was Wen who came bustling toward me half an hour after they'd entered the observation deck. Malita dragged after him as if she was being pulled by the hand. For a moment she looked like she might even have the decency to feel embarrassed. Then she smiled at me over the scent rose she was carrying—a prop that she swayed across her face with a gesture I found particularly elegant.

Wen likes anyone who's led an adventurous life. He knew all about the little comedy I was playing with Malita but he had been striking up conversations with me ever since he and Malita had become friends. Now he waved his arms at the scenery and launched into one of his impersonations of the Man of Gusto.

"This is the first time I've ever felt like I understood what Neil Armstrong meant," Wen said. "What else can you say when you look at a scene like this? 'Isn't that something?' How else could you put it? It's amazing how a trip like this can affect someone who's spent his whole life on Luna. It's been twenty years since I spent this much time Topside. We're going to be leaving the cruiser in a couple of hours—for a little side trip we've been planning—but I wanted you to know I'm going to miss having you and Shezuko with us, Joe."

The liquid sloshing in Wen's glass was a bubbly, silvery concoction I had seen him drink before. He had been afflicted with random fits of depression ever since he was a teenager. The bubbles and the silver glitter were a good indication he had chosen an active ingredient that elevated his mood. He had tried to eliminate the depression problem at one point, but he had discovered a permanent modification would affect several of the qualities he valued.

My own drink at the moment was a pleasant, mildly astringent item that was very popular on the Moon. It was laced, fortunately, with the faintest touch of a weak socializer. If it had contained anything less inhibiting, I might have started screaming.

I had spent half my remaining funds on this cruise. Malita had urged me to take it. She had called me up to discuss it. She had described the whole experience as if she was preparing a personal travelogue. She had indicated I would be part of her social circle.

I could have seen what she was doing three hours after I stepped on the cruiser. She had told me from the very beginning—on the very day I had seen her for the first time, chatting in a restaurant in Eratosthenes—that she didn't have the slightest interest in the kind of emotional adventure I could offer. Now she had apparently embarked on a campaign—and I had been doggedly ignoring all the warning signs my common sense had been pointing out. If I hadn't learned she was telling me the truth after eight months of futile efforts, she would make the pursuit so unpleasant—and costly—it would eventually become unbearable.

There is no way I can overemphasize my feelings, Malita had said. *I am not interested in emotionally intense sexual relationships. I'm not even interested in relationships in which the emotional intensity is all on one side. I've had all the emotional turbulence I want or need. I'm sorry your erotic feelings have become fixated on me. I'm sorry it's causing you discomfort and turmoil. I'm not going to let you into my life—even for a short time—merely because a random psychological process has generated feelings that you happen to consider important.*

I drew myself up and managed a socially correct look of surprise. Malita had dropped her head to her rose as soon as she had seen the emotions that had crossed my face.

"What can you possibly do out there that you can't do here?" I said.

It was a reasonable question. Wherever you go on the Moon, you're Inside and the natural environment is Outside. The important thing is making sure you're surrounded by an inside that's comfortable.

Wen's chief political adviser, Hai Jung-He, had accompanied him on the cruise. Hai had been slouching in a recliner near the "stern" of the observation deck, but he had started working his way toward us as soon as he had seen Wen was talking to me. Wen and I are both a little short by contemporary standards, so we both had to tip our heads back when he loomed over us.

Hai tended to stay in the background when Wen was socializing, but he was always there. It would have been hard not to be conscious he was there, in fact. For the first ten years of his life, Hai and his mother had lived on an income that was so close to survival level she couldn't afford optional medical services. It's my understanding the poor woman worked for one of those enterprises that attract customers by telling them real flesh and blood human females direct the responses of the simulations. By the time she could afford the appropriate treatments, her son had become a medical illustration: a human male who had responded to low gravity by developing bird bones and the kind of height that condemns you to a life of awkward tables and cramped hotel beds.

"Wen tells me he's leaving the cruiser for a side trip," I said. "Is there really anything out there that's more spectacular than the scenery we're scheduled to pass?"

Wen smiled. He leaned forward and gave me a conspiratorial pat with the back of his free hand. "We're having an adventure, Joseph. A *journalistic* adventure."

Hai frowned. A touch of consternation crossed Malita's face.

Hai lowered his head and rested his hand on Wen's shoulder. Hai was one of the most self-controlled people I had ever met, but it was obvious Wen had let his drink carry him to elevations he should have avoided.

Malita was examining me with the intense, crinkly-eyed curiosity she had directed at me on other occasions. It was a look that gave you the feeling she was noting every move you made and constructing a detailed, carefully reasoned picture of every feeling and thought that was passing through your consciousness. She had once told an interviewer her great strength was intelligence, not talent. *You really have to be endowed with a specialized talent*, she had argued, *if you want to reach the highest level in any creative field—If you want to make it into the upper one half of one percent. With intelligence, you can only work your way into the upper five or ten percent, and it usually takes an incredible effort. But the rewards can be very satisfying.*

I straightened up. I would have sacrificed the other half of my funds just to have a private farewell drink with her, but I knew I would be acting like a fool if I even suggested the idea. "It's going to be a duller trip without you, Wen. Are you going to rejoin us later?"

"We're not certain," Hai said. "Right now it looks unlikely."

Wen could slip into his politician's persona as if he was putting on a costume. He clapped me on the shoulder and his automatic responses took over. "I'll call you when we all get back to Era, Joe. I've got a little get-together planned for late next month. I think you'll find it's your kind of thing."

Shezuko shook her head when she saw me staring at Malita as they walked away. "Would it make you feel better if we played some Bach, young man?"

Shezuko had brought a small harpsichord—the kind you can rest on a table—and we had already fulfilled a minor fantasy and played together while the scenery drifted past us. Now I realized an hour with Bach was just what I needed. It would also give me an excuse to return to my cabin. Malita had knocked me into a state of shock, but I wasn't as lightheaded as Wen seemed to be. I would never recover the capital I had tossed away when I had walked into Malita's trap, but Wen's slip might help me recoup a few percent of it.

My eyes drifted toward a notably distracting young woman as I approached the elevator. I had noticed her on the first day of the cruise; she was probably the only woman on the entire passenger list who could still penetrate the mood Malita had created. She was one of those people who attract your attention because they seem to radiate health and physical opulence. The long lines of her body looked like they had been shaped by a sculptor who wanted to create a portrait of the perfect female athlete. She was so striking, in fact, that it took me a moment to realize she had been watching *me*.

I pulled out my notescreen and transmitted a memo as soon as the cabin door clicked shut. My violin had been stored in an under-the-bed drawer, cushioned by the padding provided by my highdress clothing. By the time I stood up, the cabin was advising me I had a call.

The woman whose face appeared on the wall screen called herself Chindraka Hindaja. She had contacted me a few days after I docked at Eratosthenes and shown me a blue card that proved she worked for an organization that could pay me a small retainer and a large hourly rate. She was engaged in a type of work that is sometimes referred to as "preventive peacekeeping." Her employers on Earth wanted to keep track of the things the new cities on the Moon were doing.

I am basically apolitical, but I have always believed that a technological society needs the kind of minimal international government we've developed on Earth. I've never agreed with the people who think we can let human beings colonize the Moon and the asteroids without imposing some degree of law on their activities. And it was, after all, an easy way to accumulate extra funds. Chindraka wasn't asking me to *spy* on the people I met. She just wanted information any observant gadabout might come across.

"In another three hours," Chindraka said, "you'll be a two-hour drive from Simon Razagella's hideaway. Does that sound like the kind of *adventure* Wen Kang would be interested in?"

I nodded. I didn't ask her how she knew where the hideaway was located, of course.

"Razagella's just the kind of person Wen finds irresistible," I said. "He said it was a journalistic adventure. If he's found out where Razagella's hiding, he probably thinks he can get an interview."

"I would imagine it would be a lucrative project."

Wen was the only politician I've ever met who supported himself by churning out journalism. His only political position at that time was a precarious hold on a seat in the lower tier of the Eratosthenes Legislative Assembly. The income that maintained his standard of living came from interviews, opinion pieces, travel narratives, and backlog items like his accounts of his father's adventures in the asteroid belt. Most people thought he lived off an inheritance. They didn't realize the only help he received from his ancestors was the money his mother sometimes wheedled out of the men in her life.

"He'd still have to get inside the hideaway," I said. "He's a very persuasive person, but I can't believe Razagella will hand him an interview just because he's Wen Kang."

"That's one of the things I find interesting. Wen's spent a lot of money on this pleasure trip. If he did it just so he could get an interview, he must be confident he'll be successful. There's also the question of how he found out where Razagella's located. This is the first time we've had any evidence anyone else had that information."

"He's Wen Kang. He must know half the people worth knowing on the Moon."

"It's still the kind of thing that raises questions," Chindraka said. "Would you be willing to follow them? For the usual day rate?" She smiled. "You've got the perfect cover, it seems to me."

I shook my head. She was a very intelligent woman but she had made the same mistake many people make.

"That's not my style," I said. "I don't make a nuisance of myself. It's one thing to buy a passage on this overgrown tractor just so I can maintain a normal social contact. It's another thing to go pursuing Malita across the wilderness when she's working on a private matter."

"From what I hear, Joseph, it won't make much difference anyway. You may even get to spend some extra time in her irresistible presence. It may not be the kind of contact you're most interested in, but it will be something."

I had reached my eighth decade when I fell in love with Malita, but I had only acquired two enhancements of any importance. One (as you won't be surprised to hear) provided me with almost total control over the physiological aspects of my sexual responses. That's an important matter to many women (though not all). The other enhancement was a musical performance system I purchased in the first years performance systems were available. I had been captivated by someone I still remember with great pleasure—a young entrepreneur who had enhanced her whole life when she had installed her first performance system and started playing the wooden 18th Century flute. The only people she saw after business hours were the people who played with her. I installed a system that gave me the ability to play the short-necked, lightly strung 18th Century violin and managed to join her social circle six weeks after she had first seized my imagination. I had to pay a ridiculous price for special lessons in Baroque style and performance practice, but I have never made an investment that gave me a more satisfactory return.

I have installed new information molecules in my nervous system as upgrades have become available, but I have never changed instruments. I seem to have an affinity for the music of the 18th Century.

The first time I had fallen in love I had been seven and the 21st Century had been three. There was a Frenchman once who said that love is the illusion that women differ. The more rational side of my personality sometimes tells me he may have been right; my emotions have their own opinion. Human beings are the product of a long process of natural selection. The process obviously had to favor people who respond to the opposite sex. In some of us, that tendency has been carried to an extreme —just as some people are taller or more muscular. For me, there is nothing in the entire universe more exciting than a woman—her face, the lines of her body, the intricacies of her personality.

It's true that my feelings always fade. I've never tested the area of my brain that determines your position on the monogamy-polygamy scale, but I'm confident I could predict the result. Thanks to one part of my brain structure, I live in a universe filled with dazzling, glittering women. Thanks to another part, I always know that sooner or later there will be another face, another combination of personality and physical grace....

My particular cluster of personality traits may not satisfy people who would like to fabricate the ideal human, but I have tried to satisfy my impulses without creating too much trouble for the women who capture my emotions. For most of them, the days they have spent with me haven't been that different from their encounters with other men. The only difference is the spice of the extra intensity I bring to the affair.

And haven't my adventures granted me gifts I could have acquired in no other way? I have loved architects, engineers, musicians, politicians, geologists, surgeons, athletes, economists, and women who approached activities like diving and mountaineering with the same passion I have lavished on the central concern of my life. From all of them I have learned something. The shortest route to someone's affections—male or female— is to *listen*.

But there was no way I could deny the other side of the equation. Money that had been accumulated in years had been squandered in days. Jealous rivals had pursued me. To Chindraka I was a figure of fun—a foolish man, approaching the end of his first century, who still believed he would spend the rest of his days in misery if a particular woman excluded him from her life.

I had explored most of the modification options catalogued in the databanks when I had first settled into my apartment in Eratosthenes. I had come to the Moon to escape the consequences of an exceptionally imprudent adventure. My activities had disturbed the business associates of a woman who occupied a key position in the economic rivalries that shape the affairs of the Eastern Mediterranean medical complex. For the first time in my life I found myself thinking I might have reached the limits of my capacity for turmoil.

I had once spent six weeks in the hospital, recovering from a severed spinal cord, because an unexpectedly dangerous husband pursued me down an unfamiliar road when I left his house on a motorcycle. This time, I had been forced to leave the Earth itself—my *world*, the natural home of mankind!—because I had received a well-worded threat from an organization that possessed a formidable capacity to carry it out. Wasn't it time I faced the fact that one of my escapades was eventually going to culminate in a disaster that couldn't be repaired?

I didn't have to weaken my responses to women, of course. That would be the simplest and least expensive modification, but there were other possibilities. I could choose the same modification Shezuko had picked. I could even eliminate my feelings for a particular person and leave my basic personality intact. That would be a slightly risky, exceptionally expensive option, but it was probably possible.

I had been toying with the possibilities for over a year when I had encountered Malita and the initial rush of excitement had pushed the idea out of my head. It had been almost three months before I had admitted I was staring at a woman who had surrounded herself with a seamless glass wall.

I had been living for exactly seven years and five months the first time I had been tormented by the emotions Malita had evoked. Was I going to be experiencing this kind of gloom and misery two hundred years from now? Or a thousand?

Fortunately, Shezuko didn't harass me with nagging attempts to convert me to her view. We were both feeling quite relaxed, in fact, as we drove across the lunar landscape toward the obscure crater in which "informed sources" claimed Simon Razagella had built his hermitage. Our hour with Bach had been followed by the kind of easy, utterly tensionless sexual interlude both of us found comforting. The only undiplomatic thought she mentioned was her surprise that I was following Wen and Malita. Unlike Chindraka, she knew that wasn't my style.

"Has Malita really affected you that much?" Shezuko said. "I know we're talking about feelings that are inherently irrational, but it seems to me you're dealing with someone who's made it very clear she's going to make things as unpleasant as she can."

Just to my left, through the dust floating around our windows, I could see the tracks Wen's vehicle had pressed into the ground. As far as I could tell, no one else had ever passed this way. The population of the Moon had just reached twenty million in those days. Most lunarians still lived in six cities.

Like Casanova, I usually respond to faces. This time it had been the movements of Malita's hands that had caught my eye. I hadn't known she was Malita Trevari Divora when I had glanced across that restaurant and seen her relaying some bit of gossip to her friends. I just knew I had never seen hands that moved with that much animation and intelligence.

It had been forty years since Malita had created *The Saga of the Six*. It had been thirty-five years since her husband had died. She was striking at me with such force, I suspected, precisely because she associated me with the same attitudes that had led Pin Divora to his death. She had spent the first ten years of her adult life under the spell of a man who believed he should surrender to every impulse without reservation. How could she lower her defenses for a man who was willing to sacrifice almost anything merely because a particular woman had temporarily activated his emotional programming?

If you download Malita's original version of *Six* today, it looks crude by contemporary standards. The imaging techniques seem primitive. The characterization programs seem skimpy and over-consistent. *Six* captured the imagination of a huge public primarily because Malita had zeroed in on the moral implications of personality modification at a time when people were just becoming aware that another new technology was about to disrupt their lives. The work she had put on the market since then had been less successful commercially. You couldn't view it, however, without realizing it had been fabricated by a personality that had emerged from a turbulent youth with its buoyant, probing rationality still intact.

I could have told Shezuko I had known hundreds of women in my life and I had never met anyone as alive as Malita seemed to be. I could have told her that the young woman who had eyed me on the observation deck had been a more exciting physical specimen than Malita, but nothing in her face had communicated the sensitivity and wisdom I saw in the looks Malita bestowed on the people who attracted her attention. And even as I talked, I would have wondered if I would have seen any of that sensitivity and wisdom if my mother's body had washed another combination of chemicals across my brain cells when I had been developing in her womb.

Is there any difference between a personality shaped by chance and a personality shaped by conscious choice? Is one more "real" than the other?

Instead, I changed the subject by showing Shezuko how some of the terrain we passed looked to an experienced climber. One of the pleasanter adventures of my life had been a season with a woman who was a specialist in implanted skill systems. She had acquired a passion for climbing but she had never enhanced her own climbing skills. I had thought I would have to buy a climbing implant when I fell in love with her, but it hadn't been necessary. She had responded as soon as she saw how I felt and she had enjoyed teaching me the rudiments of her avocation. We had spent almost three months together and she had taught me some of the fine points of the tradeoffs you should take into account when you consider an enhancement. My musical implant, for example, affects the fine motor activity in my left hand and the large muscles in my bow arm. The muscles would adjust if I acquired an implant that turned me into a boxer, but I probably couldn't pursue music and boxing at the same time.

Razagella had concealed his refuge in the rim of a nameless crater that was approximately three kilometers in diameter. A secondary meteor strike had opened a narrow gap in one section of the rim wall. To enter the crater, you had to work your way through a boulder field while you watched for treacherous dips in the surface level.

We stopped about a kilometer from the squat little door that Razagella had installed in one of the more rugged areas of the rim wall. The dust cloud that surrounded our vehicle floated to the ground. I peered though the window and picked out the tracks that passed us on our left and terminated at the door.

Razagella had burrowed into the side of the wall at a point where it was almost vertical. On the right, about two hundred meters from the door, a big freight hauler had been parked under an overhang. There were no markings on the side of the box.

Shezuko pointed toward a spot somewhere on my left. "It looks like Wen and your current model of female perfection aren't the only people making a visit."

"What makes you think that?"

"Follow the hauler's tracks. They don't go anywhere near the door and they cross Wen's tracks right over there. It looks to me like the hauler made its tracks after Wen drove up to the door. It could be the hauler Razagella used when he moved here, but I don't think he's the kind who'd leave a tell-tale like that lying around."

I nodded. I'm no expert on reading tracks, but the hauler had obviously pressed across Wen's tracks after his tractor had approached the cliff. I was also aware that the garage on the other side of the door already housed the only vehicle Razagella had used when he had decided to abandon civilization. Chindraka had thoughtfully furnished me with a detailed diagram of Razagella's layout "just in case you happen to get inside."

I pulled out my notescreen and started writing a description of the situation. "I've got some friends in an office in Eratosthenes," I said. "Maybe they can tell us something about the hauler."

Shezuko stared at me. I had sounded too nonchalant, of course.

"Without any markings to go on?" Shezuko said. "Those must be some friends."

Chindraka responded in text—as I'd requested—several long minutes after I'd transmitted my message. Her employers had apparently added surveillance capabilities to the international communication satellites that orbited the Moon. Once she knew a particular vehicle might be of interest, she could order a search of the recordings collected during the last hundred hours.

The hauler had been backtracked across the wilderness we had just crossed. It had started its journey in Copernicus—a fact that was so interesting she could offer me a substantial bonus if I talked my way into Razagella's bunker and told her who his unknown visitors were.

It wasn't hard to follow her thinking. Wen might be a minor member of his legislature, but he had important connections. He would be a perfect go-between if the ruling faction in Eratosthenes wanted to arrange a private conference with the families that dominated the Copernican industrial complex.

It was a tempting proposal, but I'm proud to say I rejected the idea as soon as I saw it. If Wen was arranging some kind of political deal, that was his business. The woman on the other side of Razagella's door was—at that moment anyway—the most talented and accomplished woman who had ever enthralled me. If I accepted Chindraka's offer, I would know, beyond a doubt, that I would never spend a happy moment with her.

Hai pinged us just as I was reaching for the tractor's control interface. He nodded knowingly as soon as he popped onto the screen and saw me looking back at him.

"I see you decided to visit us, Joe."

"I'm afraid I yielded to an impulse."

"Would you like to join our party? Wen is interviewing Dr. Razagella right now, but he and Malita both said I should tell you they'd love to see you."

It was an ironic situation. Wen, Malita, and Razagella were, in fact, already prisoners. Hai would have been better off if I had carried out my intent and driven over the horizon. Instead, he had immediately decided I was going to hang around Razagella's doorstep and make a nuisance of myself. Like most men who are fascinated by politics, Hai didn't understand people who pursue pleasure and emotional adventure.

"Malita's been talking about you ever since we left the cruiser," Hai said. "Personally, I think she's beginning to feel guilty about the way we left you behind like that."

There used to be a saying to the effect that all the world loves a lover. It would be more accurate to say most people think my kind of feelings are a subject of comedy. The dry, mocking tone that colored Hai's words had followed me around since I was a teenager. It didn't occur to me he was lying. I didn't realize there was anything wrong until we climbed out of our tractor inside the garage and Hai ushered us into Razagella's living quarters.

Malita, Wen, and Razagella were sitting on a low, unpadded bench that Razagella had roughed out of a rock. The young woman who had eyed me in the cruiser was leaning against a wall. She was watching the couch with a small, unfriendly smile playing across her face.

The door clicked shut behind us. "I have two pieces of information," Hai said. "First—don't try to activate your emergency implants. This instrument I'm holding in my hand can transform the message into useless nonsense at any range up to a hundred meters. It also transmits a signal that can transform the attempt to send an emergency call into a painful experience. Wen has already found that out. Second—don't be misled by the fact that we aren't carrying weapons. Denko can handle all five of you barehanded. Our simulations indicate it would take her about three minutes to kill every one of you, assuming you made the best use of the best combat skills you are known to possess."

Wen was glaring at him defiantly. His hands were shoved inside the pockets of his jacket and he was bending forward as if he was pressing his forehead against an invisible spring. Malita looked like a queen. Her back was as straight as a laser beam, but there was nothing rigid about the lines of her body. She could have been sitting on the observation deck of the cruiser, hands folded in her lap, calmly observing the landscape.

Razagella was staring at the floor. Fifteen years ago Hai would have been forced to keep him in chains. Now he was utterly defenseless. He had removed all his combat enhancements and he had deliberately avoided exercise and let his natural strength atrophy.

It was the first time I had ever seen Razagella. Like everyone else who had ever met him, I was surprised to discover he looked so commonplace.

It made sense when you thought about it, of course. He had evaded the manhunters on Hochheim precisely because he possessed the best safeguard an undercover agent could own: the ability to fade into a crowd. The glamour that surrounded his name had been bestowed on him after the Kumari *raj* had decided it might be best, after all, if it yielded to his demands and gave up its attempt to dominate the wealthiest city in Earth orbit.

The walls of the room were painted off-white. The only decoration was a small wall-mounted video. Razagella had spent the last ten years of his life working in a Copernican charity hospital that offered help to people like Hai's mother. Apparently that hadn't been good enough. He was still trying to appease the part of his conscience that objected to the things he had done on Hochheim.

"I'm sorry to inform you my friend Hai has betrayed my trust," Wen said. "He's apparently made a lucrative deal with one of the great humanitarian families that run Copernicus. According to what he's told me, the hauler outside contains a complete personality modification facility and two accredited technicians. Sometime during the next two days, I'm supposed to become a secret traitor, too."

Malita was regarding me with a look that was so hostile it provoked a rush of emotion that took me by surprise. Even then, when I was still adjusting to the discovery I had stepped into a very dangerous situation, she could make me feel that her approval was the only thing in the universe that mattered.

"I told Hai that couldn't possibly be you in that vehicle," Malita said.

Hai smiled. "Apparently she didn't understand you as well as I did."

Hai was more of a political theorist than I had realized. By the time we had been standing there five minutes, I had heard most of the details of his scheme and managed to fill in two thirds of the blanks he left empty. Wen was an ideal choice for the kind of modification the Copernicans had in mind. Most of the important details of Wen's private life were part of the public record. Any competent expert in modification procedures could have guessed his whole life had been shaped by a childhood in which he had been neglected by a glamorous mother who maintained her contacts with the wealthy and powerful by engaging in a series of sexual involvements. Wen's glare became angrier and angrier as Hai talked, but we all knew Hai was explicating the obvious. The technicians in the hauler would have no problem developing an approach that would give them the kind of control they wanted. It's my understanding, for example, that they could have linked Wen's anger at his mother with a female controller who would have functioned as a rival-avenger.

But there was no question the procedure would take the full two days Hai had allotted. That kind of modification would normally take weeks if the technicians were working with an involuntary subject whose personal history was less accessible. Hai had dragged me inside because he couldn't let a bumptious intruder set him back two hours. If Wen and Malita spent more than fifty or sixty hours with Razagella, someone might become suspicious.

"He's already told us what he's going to do to the rest of us," Malita said. "We're all going to leave here with pleasant, innocuous memories— the kind no one would ever think of questioning."

Hai smiled. "Perhaps we'll give Joe the memory he most wants. We could even give it to you, too, Malita. That would solve both your problems, wouldn't it? He'd have what he wants. And you wouldn't have to listen to him scraping that violin every time you think you're going to enjoy a little peace."

I turned around and stared up at him. I could have broken his arms merely by squeezing them with my hands.

The woman, Denko, rested her fingers on my shoulder. She had slipped away from the wall the moment I had started to turn.

Was I angry at Hai because he had suggested that the memory of a single act could satisfy the kind of profound, complex emotional hungers a woman like Malita could arouse? Or was I ready to choke the life out of him because he had ridiculed an art that may be the primary evidence our species deserves to survive?

"Remind me to buy you an enhancement for your hearing," I said. "I'm afraid they don't sell enhancements for the soul."

Denko's fingers slid toward my neck. I turned around, maintaining my dignity, and found Shezuko smiling at me.

"I regret to say I feel forced to disagree with you," Shezuko said. "The enhancement you're referring to is called music."

Wen and Simon Razagella were both staring at us. We were babbling, of course. But it was the kind of babbling that would impress a romantic like Wen. It probably impressed Razagella more than he would have admitted. In spite of all his claims that he wanted to live a life of harmless isolation, some part of Razagella's psyche still responded to displays of gallantry and bravado. He hadn't completely eliminated the young man who had dreamed of doing great deeds.

He was still trying, of course. The small video on the wall had flickered once every thirty seconds since we had entered the room. Now, when it flickered again, I finally realized what it was. Razagella was displaying—one frame at a time—the complete record of the riot that had taken place when he had shut down the programs that controlled the life support system in the Hotel von Braun.

Malita shook her head. "It's too bad Joe didn't become fixated on you, Shezu. You make a better couple than he and I ever would."

"I don't think the quality of the pairing is Joe's primary consideration," Wen said. "As I understand it, Joe has chosen to follow a particular impulse wherever it leads him—in the belief the rewards are worth almost any sacrifice. He feels a passion for a particular individual adds a priceless quality to a relationship with a member of the opposite sex. The things he does with the object of his desire may not be very different from the things he might do with someone else, but they *feel* different because of the emotions she has aroused. Is that a fair summary of your attitudes, Joe?"

"It's almost a direct quote. I didn't realize you understood me so well."

Razagella was smiling. It was a thin smile, but he was clearly enjoying our attempts at insouciance.

"I find it intriguing that Joe's dominant passion has been paired with a subordinate passion for music," Razagella said. "Isn't there a tradition that the male courts the female with displays of singing and dancing?"

"It's an interesting notion," Hai said. "You'll have to discuss it without my former employer's contributions. Denko will escort you to the hauler, Wen. I know she's unarmed. I know you've realized she's operating with a handicap, since we can't damage you physically. It would still be best if you followed her instructions."

Denko had returned to her position against the wall. From the neck down, she looked relaxed and almost languid. From the neck up, she was a wary, wide-eyed predator whose brain was registering every move we made.

"Just stand up and start down the hall," Hai said. "She'll fall in behind and tell you where to go next."

Wen stood up, but there was nothing compliant about the way he moved. It's hard to communicate contempt when you have to look up at someone, but he managed to do it. He was one of those people, I think, who have never admitted anything can defeat them.

He had some feeling for tactics, too. He didn't go on the offensive until he was only two steps from Hai.

Hai managed to evade both of Wen's kicks but that was the best he could do. With his physique, he couldn't block or counterattack without hurting himself. Denko had glided toward Wen as soon as he had deviated from a plain walk, but another factor came into play before she could reach him. Razagella had grabbed a small bag Malita had laid on the floor—it was the only loose object in the room—and tossed it at Denko's legs. Then he flowed out of his chair and launched himself at her waist with the practiced skill of someone who had spent his whole life in low gravity environments. He had removed his enhancements but his body still remembered a few things.

The sight that truly thrilled me—the image that still stops my heart when I think of it—was the way Malita followed him across the room.

This was the first time in her entire life that she had engaged in a real act of violence. The only martial art she had ever studied had been a simplified form of aikido—a tradition that tends to attract people who want to nullify attacks without inflicting serious damage on their adversaries. Yet, when the hour came, she didn't hesitate. Underneath her pose of contemptuous indifference, she was burning with outrage.

A small alteration of your memory may seem like a minor matter. Malita still thought of herself as an artist. Memory and personality were the primary source of the unique qualities that gave her work its value.

Shezuko joined the melee as soon as she saw the other three were making a serious effort. Hai's analysis had been a precise forecast of the future. Denko could have killed all four of them in three minutes. She was hampered, however, by the need to keep them alive and unharmed. In forty-eight hours, we were all supposed to leave Razagella's hideaway in a state that would arouse no comment from anyone.

I hadn't memorized the plan Chindraka had transmitted, but I did remember one fact. Thirty meters from the room I was standing in, at the end of a short tunnel, there was an emergency airlock. Razagella might be semi-suicidal, but he hadn't overlooked one of the elementary precautions of lunar living.

I turned away from the action just as Denko landed a kick that made Shezuko double over in agony. I had been living on the Moon for almost two years but I still hadn't acquired all the automatic responses I needed. I took three stumbling, Earth-type steps before I remembered where I was and switched to a clumsy version of the long, land-on-your-toes strides that are the lunar equivalent of running. Hai yelled at me as I reached the airlock, and I looked back and saw him flying toward me.

He didn't try to follow me inside the airlock after I closed the hatch behind me. Instead, he stared at me through the window as he unfolded a telescoping electrical shock stick.

"You're being stupid," Hai said. "You're the one person in this group we can afford to kill. Nobody will ask a single question if you happen to have an accident."

I waited for him to come in, but he had apparently decided it would be too risky, even with the stick in his hand. I turned my attention to the emergency suits stored on the wall, and we eyed each other as I prepared myself for the moment when the outer hatch would swing open.

The emergency suits were simple skin-tights, but you would have known they were top quality even if you hadn't recognized the trademark printed on the hangers. The one I chose went on as if it had been designed by the best tailor I had ever commissioned. The interface utilized the unmistakable voice of one of my favorite actresses—an impeccably patrician woman who offered me reassuring bits of data as she talked me through the donning procedure. The recycling system would keep me alive for three hours and twenty-two minutes, I was advised. The repair system could mend 107 centimeters of gashes and rips—eleven centimeters more than the industry standard.

It took me ninety-one seconds to finish donning, according to the time strip over the hanger. Then I opened the outer hatch and stepped onto the Topside of Luna for the first time since I had left Earth.

The emergency implants we use today are probably ten times stronger than the implants we used then. Hai had said his jammer could block out the signal as long as we were located within a hundred meters of it, and I had no trouble believing him. Even if I managed to transmit a clear, unspoiled signal, the nearest receiving station would probably receive a weak blip. My secret weapon was my relationship with Chindraka. If she was doing her job as well as she seemed to be doing it, the rescue system would have been advised it should give her a ping the moment it received a call from the precious, infinitely valuable body of her devoted agent, Joseph Louis Baske.

There was a small boulder field off to the right. It looked to me like the closest rock in the group was located at least a hundred and twenty meters from the wall of the crater. I might be out of Hai's range before I reached it, but I wasn't going to take the chance. No one had contradicted Hai when he had claimed his device could transform an emergency signal into a burst of pain.

It was the first time I had made any serious attempt to run while I was wearing a skin-tight. I was so engrossed in the effort I didn't realize I was already in trouble. Hai had alerted the people in the hauler. The cab had detached itself from the box while I was still inside the airlock.

If I ever find myself involved in a war, I hope I can arrange things so I can fight on a world that has equipped itself with an atmosphere. The worst thing about the whole situation was the fact that I couldn't hear anything. I wouldn't have known the cab was coming after me, in fact, if Hai hadn't decided to transmit a few words over the intersuit radio.

"The driver of the cab has one of these magic wands, too, Joe. He's over on your left and it looks to me like he's going to have you in range well before you get a hundred meters from me. The pain hits you with a real jolt. Wen dropped to his knees as soon as it cut in."

I couldn't look over my shoulder without running the risk I might fall. I didn't see the cab until I bumbled into the boulder field and positioned myself in the middle of three rocks that were all about Hai's height.

The cab had already moved into range. It couldn't enter the boulder field, but it didn't have to. The field was so small an experienced moonhiker could have crossed it in three long strides. If I tried to run into the open, the driver could just circle the rocks and stay near me.

I am not a physically courageous person. I have, however, developed some of the responses a human male with my tendencies needs to acquire. My legs started moving before my brain had realized it had made a decision. Once again, I found myself traveling through a silent world in which all the important facts were hidden from my senses.

I had veered away from the boulder field at an angle that made it look like I was trying to run out of the crater. I didn't start running toward the crater wall until I reached a place where the ground was covered with treacherous-looking pits. Then I twisted sharply to the right, as if I had just seen the pits and decided to avoid them.

It was one of those times when you have to ignore the inner voice that's advising you you're doing something incredibly stupid. My only justification for heading for the rim wall was its height. The summit was a good hundred and fifty meters above me at this point. If Hai had been telling the truth, a hundred meters *up* should be just as good as a hundred meters on the horizontal.

I had climbed a few rock formations without ropes or special equipment on Earth, but I had done it in the company of an experienced woman who had picked a viable route before we started out. All I knew at that moment was the general layout of the lowest section of the wall directly in front of me. I would have to start the climb by working my way up a vertical cliff face that ended about fifteen meters above my eye level. Above that, there was a short slope that looked like it could be covered on all fours, if you were careful. After that, I would just have to hope I could pick my way upward.

I grew up on a planet that has been carved by wind and water. To an eye trained in that kind of environment, a landscape shaped by meteor impacts seems as patternless as a sandbox kicked by an angry child. As far as I was concerned, the crater wall was a jumble of bumpy surfaces, randomly located rocks, chaotically placed outcroppings, and slopes that alternated between the suicidal and the just-negotiable without any discernible reason why they should be either one.

I crept up the initial vertical by feeling my way along one handhold or toehold at a time, the same way I would have climbed a similar face on Earth. The low lunar gravity gave me a small advantage but the days when I could play Superhero Earth Man had ended months ago. I had been on the Moon almost two years. My muscles had responded in the customary manner.

Hai came back on the intersuit system when I was pressed against the face of the wall about three good holds from the top of the vertical. "There are missile weapons in the cab, Joe. We're not interested in killing you if we don't have to, but no one will have any trouble believing you fell. It's exactly the kind of accident that happens to someone who's spent his life trying to impress women."

The cab had parked at the foot of the wall, where I could give it a few panicky glances as I tried to concentrate on the lumps and indentations that had become my chief interest in life. No one stepped onto the surface while I struggled up the rest of the vertical. The people in the hauler were supposed to be technicians, not killers. If they wanted to threaten me with artillery, they could take it out and let me see it.

I bit back the impulse to tell him that. If silence could unnerve me, maybe it could unnerve Hai, too.

I started crawling up the first incline, and the suit warned me it had repaired a small rip before I had covered a full meter. The inclines looked safer than the verticals, but they were treacherous. The "soil" of Topside is a gritty, lumpy blanket of dust and rubble that has been pounded by big meteor strikes and ground by the millions of microscopic particles that fall on every square meter of the Moon as the eons go by. The dust created a slippery surface that had to be treated with caution. The grit contained needles that could cut through the suit if they encountered it at the right angle. If I reached for a protruding bit of rock to steady myself, I had to wiggle it before I put my weight on it. Half the rocks I tested pulled free of the blanket at the first jiggle.

By the time I reached the top of the incline, the suit had given me at least four warnings. "You have 96 centimeters of repairs left," the famous voice said. "You seem to be engaging in a hazardous form of behavior. I must advise you that Keradino Luna cannot assume legal responsibility if you persist in your present pattern. The suit you are wearing is designed to provide you with minimal support while you await rescue. The warranty cannot cover sustained high levels of activity."

I paused at the bottom of another vertical and looked over the ground below me before I planned my next moves. Hai's friends were still sitting in the cab but I lost interest in their activities as soon as my peripheral vision jerked my attention toward the area around Razagella's emergency airlock. Denko was flowing across the landscape as if she was made out of whipped cream.

It seems strange, nowadays, that I hadn't realized what she was as soon as I saw her. It's hard to believe there was a time, only a few decades ago, when people like her were a novelty. We all knew it was possible to design a human being gene by gene.

It was obvious oligarchs like the Copernican families had the resources to provide themselves with bodyguards, servants, sex partners, and any other kind of customized specialists they thought they needed. We just hadn't gotten used to the idea that some of them were actually doing it.

She stopped when she reached the foot of the wall, and Hai gave me another speech. "Keep your eyes on the tableau below you, Joe. In a moment, you'll see the cab making its departure. In a few minutes, it will be outside the crater. Don't assume you can slip over the top of the rim and dash down the outside slope. By the time you get to the top of the rim, the cab will be placed where it can move along the outside slope and stay with you if you try to leave us that way. I'm afraid you're caught in a pincer. If you stay on this side of the wall, Denko doesn't even have to climb all the way up. She just has to get high enough to maintain the appropriate distance."

If I had been a true hero of derring-do, I wouldn't have hesitated for a moment. But Hai's words brought me to a temporary halt. I had, in fact, been hoping I could go over the top of the rim and take advantage of the peculiarities of the lunar landscape. The outside of most lunar crater walls is a long, gentle slope, like a giant dune. If I made it to the top, I could hurry down the other side while Denko was still working her way up the inside.

A lunar vehicle, on the other hand, could climb halfway up the outside slope. I would have gone to all this trouble for nothing.

The cab backed away from the wall, as promised, but Denko stayed where she was when I returned to my labors. She didn't start climbing, in fact, until I was halfway up the second vertical. I had been assuming she was an expert in anything that involved physical skill. I began to feel a glimmer of hope when I looked down and discovered she seemed to be proceeding gracefully but slowly—like an inexperienced climber with a huge natural talent. Was it possible Hai's superwoman hadn't received any training in the alpine arts? Had they assumed she would just be a mayhem expert who operated under Topside?

I looked ahead of me and began to plan a route that would edge me to the left as I climbed. As Hai had noted, Denko didn't have to pursue me all the way to the summit. If she stopped when she was only fifty meters above the bottom of the wall, she would still have me in range when I reached the top. If I could put some horizontal distance between us too, on the other hand, I could still create a hundred meter gap.

I had one big advantage over her. I was used to reading cliff faces and working out routes. She was mostly following my route—and doing it with sensible caution.

The moment of decision came when I was still about fifteen meters below the summit. I had just reached the bottom of the last vertical. Denko was inching her way along a face I had negotiated a few minutes earlier. The distance between us was about ninety meters—perhaps ninety-five. It was obvious the gap was as big as it was going to get.

Hai had said a hundred meters. Wasn't it possible he had exaggerated the range when he had talked to us? Hadn't he proved he thought lying was a legitimate tactic?

I found two well braced rocks and held on. The verbal trigger I had chosen for my emergency implant was easy to remember. It was the name, pronounced backward, of the girl who had first activated another response when I had been seven.

The pain tore a scream out of me as soon as I finished the last syllable. My legs thrashed against the lunar surface. The voice of the famous actress advised me I had destroyed another ten centimeters of valuable material and now had only forty centimeters in reserve.

As all military experts know, a well-timed diversion can be just as valuable as more heroic maneuvers (and I will let you imagine how I acquired my insight into military matters). Hai had been forced to take Denko's place when he had decided she had to pursue me up the rim wall. He couldn't leave his prisoners alone in the room that contained Razagella's primary communications setup.

Malita had been the only prisoner still standing up when Hai had entered the room with his shock stick. Shezu had been lying on the floor, curled around the stomach blow she had received just before I started running. Wen and Razagella had both been unconscious, and Denko had bound them with their own clothes for good measure. Malita had been cowering in a corner with her arms dangling humbly by her sides, and she had stayed there while Hai exchanged messages with Denko. She didn't break from her corner until she knew I had failed.

It should have been an uneven contest. Malita had settled for a form of aikido that had been designed for people who were interested in a rudimentary form of self-defense. Hai had studied one of the classic schools of stick fighting and he was armed with a stick that could deliver crippling jolts of pain if it merely brushed his opponent.

For all his cleverness, fortunately, Hai had forgotten the great military axiom called the Principle of the Objective. He protected himself against threats to his person and forgot Malita was really interested in the jammer clipped to his belt. Once she got that away from him, the flick of a button gave her the only opportunity she needed.

She was a little surprised when the person who responded to her emergency signal was an obscure international bureaucrat named Chindraka Hindaja. I was surprised myself. Chindraka had placed a flag on any call for help that came from anyone located within fifty kilometers of Razagella's crater.

In spite of all the traditions of romantic fiction, it's been my experience that heroic feats are an overrated form of courtship. There was a brief moment of camaraderie after I staggered into the airlock and we all babbled and clutched while we waited for the rescue party. It took me about five minutes to realize most of the applause was being directed at Malita. Joe, it seemed, had done something he was good at—all that experience at evading irate husbands and lovers really does come in handy, doesn't it? ha, ha—and Malita had done something unexpected and incredibly brave.

"I couldn't believe it when Malita told me what she'd done," Wen said as we stood in front of the airlock window, big grins stretching our faces, and watched Hai and his co-conspirators lumber out of the crater in their hauler. "And I had to be unconscious through the whole thing. She was fighting for our lives three steps from where I was lying and I may as well have been on Earth. And you climbing the rim wall, too. That must have been rough."

Two weeks after I returned from Razagella's hideaway, I turned away from a session with the databanks and realized I had actually pared my modification options to a two-item short list. I could pick the same option Shezuko had chosen, or I could go for a more elaborate procedure that would temper my feelings as soon as I encountered a certain level of resistance. The second approach would require careful, precise, very expensive work. On the other hand, it would obviously be a cost-effective measure over the long term.

It was a shock to realize I had gone that far. This wasn't the first time I had been forced to admit that one of my inamoratas would never smile at me across a dinner table or move inside my arms. It doesn't happen that often, I'm happy to say, but it does happen, and I had learned that my basic nature eventually reasserts itself. In a year—perhaps two, in this case—a face or a flash of hair would attract my attention. I would feel my pulse quickening ever so slightly. Something would stir under the huge black weight that had been pressing on my emotions.

It had always worked that way in the past, anyway. This time I had been catapulted back to the state I had been in when I first arrived on the Moon. There were moments when I stopped dead in the middle of my apartment and cringed as I relived the pain and terror that had followed my attempt to use my emergency implant.

I might have taken some comfort, I suppose, from the thought that the whole episode proves that personalities with my sexual orientation have some social value. If I hadn't been hanging around the edges of Wen Kang's life, the pleasantest city on the Moon would have become the victim of a major political conspiracy.

My achievement was, of course, even grander than I realized. If I had been endowed with a different personality structure, the citizens of Wen's city couldn't have turned to a leader who could rally a stubborn, pugnacious resistance when the Copernican oligarchs attempted to annex Eratosthenes in 2108. Wen would have been an agent of the Copernicans instead.

I didn't know Wen's ultimate destiny at the time, and I'm not sure it would have made any difference if I had. The political affairs of mankind were not my primary interest.

Casanova was seventy-three when he died—and he had spent the last fourteen years of his life in semi-retirement, composing his memoirs and earning a stipend as a duke's librarian. I was seventy-four. Would Casanova have chosen more decades of turbulence if they had been offered to him? Was there, after all, a limit to the human organism's capacity for adventure?

Step into the shop. Trim a little here. Add something there. How many pleasures can you enjoy when you're dead?

I responded with some suspicion, naturally, when my apartment advised me I had a call from a woman who had nearly killed me.

She was, as you might expect, a very straightforward person. "I've been given a tenday off," she said, after I offered her a carefully neutral greeting. "I'm calling to see if you'd like to have dinner with me. This evening. If you can."

I've spent a big part of my life watching for certain signs. In her case, they were written all over her: In the way she bent toward the camera, in the lines of her face, in the way her clothes looked like they had been selected with too much thought and arranged with too much care. My intrepid exploit might not have impressed the sorceress who controlled my emotional state, but it had apparently affected someone.

It wasn't the first time a woman had developed a passion for the rather unremarkable combination of physical traits and personal quirks that I bear around with me. Usually I try to accommodate them. I've been in the other position so many times I would be a monster if I didn't have some sympathy for their plight.

With Denko, obviously, there were other considerations that had to be taken into account. "As I remember it," I said, "the last time I saw you, you were deliberately doing things that could have truncated my lifespan."

She shrugged—more nervously (even shyly) than she might have under other circumstances. "It was just business. It was one of the last things I wanted to do, Mr. Baske… Joe."

"But you didn't have any choice, I gather?"

"There are some things I have to do. Just like you do some things."

"And now I'm supposed to assume you just want to see me for the pleasure of it? You don't have to do something you aren't mentioning?"

"I talked to… the person I report to… before I left. She said to tell you there are no problems. They know you're not a meddler. She said to tell you that anyone who understands you would have known Hai should have let you leave the crater. Instead of thinking he had to invite you inside."

"She sounds like a very perceptive woman."

"She is! She told me I could come here if I wanted to, but I should understand you might not be interested. She said I should understand you're basically interested in the way women make you feel. Not the way they feel about you."

There was something charmingly naive about her. She was holding her hands in front of her as if she was pleading with me. Her eyes had a confused, trapped look. I didn't know how old she was, but I was confident she was coping with emotions that had never troubled her before.

"We can meet in the most public place you want," Denko said. "You can take any precautions you want. I can even pay for a complete personal security check. If that's what you want."

It wasn't a totally impossible proposal. This time, after all, we would be meeting in a city, not an isolated wilderness, and we would be surrounded by police officers and handy communications devices. If I arranged for some kind of continuous monitoring of my whereabouts and my vital signs.…

"You're asking quite a lot, Denko. I'm not a very brave person. You shouldn't judge me by our last interaction. I've just about concluded, in fact, that I may have used up my capacity for taking risks. I nearly died on that rim wall. I know you didn't have any control over your actions, but I've been living for the last two weeks with the knowledge that I couldn't have stopped myself if I had surrendered to the pain burning though my nervous system. I would have slid all the way to the bottom, with grit and rocks tearing at my suit, and probably used up the last centimeters I had left in the repair system. Even if we do meet in a public place, I probably won't want to be alone with you later."

"It can be as public as you want. I understand. My supervisor warned me you might feel that way. She said it's something I'm going to have to learn to live with. It would be nice if you could pick a place where they'll let you play your violin. But that's up to you. It can be any place you want."

I stared at her. It was, in many ways, the most bizarre conversation I've ever participated in.

"You want me to bring my violin?"

She swallowed. The anxiety signs I had picked up before jumped from subtle to outright flashing.

"I saw you play. On the cruiser. With your friend. Shezuko."

I probably wouldn't have understood if I had been thirty years younger. As it was, it took me several seconds to put it together. Then I almost threw my head back and laughed. Even after all these years—after all the times my life has been bedeviled by a smile or the dance of a pair of hands—I could still be surprised when it happened to someone else.

"You don't know what you look like… Joe. When you play. I couldn't stop watching you. The second time—I was supposed to be getting ready to leave the cruiser. I watched you right up to the last second I had."

I've experienced fifty more adventures since then (approximately—I don't keep count). Some have been just as gloomy and unrewarding as my encounter with Malita. All have been more stimulating emotionally than the days I spent with Denko. She was a pleasant, sensual woman, as I had thought she would be, but her emotional responses were limited—and she certainly didn't arouse any storms of passion on my side of the relationship. Yet in the end, for all her limitations, it was Denko—not Malita, not any of the others—who lured me away from the temptations of the semi-suicide peddled by the modification establishments. When I think about my time with Denko, I remember two things: the blinding physical climaxes her body could produce, and the hours I spent playing for her—just for her, with no other audience.

She was a child of the laboratory. Every aspect of her personality, in theory, had been charted and measured. Her ability to fight and kill on behalf of her creators was supposed to be her only reason for existence. Yet she could sit in my apartment for hours at a time, hypnotized by the way a dedicated dilettante drew complicated patterns of sound from four strings, a bow, and a soundbox.

Over the years I have met a number of musicians who share my fascination with Bach's sonatas for the unaccompanied violin. The sonatas are something of a cult item, in fact. They are thorny, they are difficult, they are incredibly challenging. No one would claim they are a pleasure in any normal sense of the word. Very few people enjoy listening to them. Musicians return to them, over and over, because we have learned that we discover something new every time we explore their complexities. There is no end to their mysteries—just as there is no end to the mysteries of the human personality.

ROMANCE IN EXTENDED TIME

She was beautiful, young, intelligent, witty,
highly cultivated, well read, and a power in Rome.
—Giacomo Casanova, *History of My Life*, tr. Willard R. Trask

I didn't hear the three missiles strike when they landed on the rear wheel of our vehicle. The missiles were drops of plastic with just enough mass to make it through the air, and they were moving at a relatively low speed—about ninety meters per second, I would guess. On a low-gravity planet like Mercury, a modest muzzle velocity will give you all the range you need for most practical purposes.

At the moment the missiles hit, I was lounging on a reclining chair, under an awning that protected me from bird droppings, falling insects, and other woodland indignities. I was taking some pleasure in the fact that my accommodations were a sizable improvement over the closets spaceships offer their passengers.

I was traveling at a leisurely pace through an idealized temperate-zone forest composed of well-spaced, aesthetically varied three-hundred-meter trees. My conveyance had been purchased from an owner who had stocked the refrigerator and the wine chest with a connoisseur's selection of prefabricated food and wine. The fabrication unit situated near the rear wheel had been equipped with programs that could produce several hundred items that were supposed to be just as palatable as the champagne I was currently holding in my hand.

On my left—where I could give it an occasional politely conversational glance—there was a face that displayed an intriguing interplay of two themes: sensuality and alertness. Ling Chime's features were round and fleshy, but her genetic designer had tempered the fleshiness with a sharp nose, high cheekbones, and eyes that seemed to be constantly dancing around the landscape. On my right the Elector—Ling's employer—was dispensing genuinely entertaining gossip about the world of the arts. I was even willing to admit that the Elector was just as attractive as Ling was, in her large-scaled, arm-waving way.

The whole scene was permeated, in addition, with a pleasant touch of the exotic—the light that created peculiar, inconsistent shadows under the trees. The ecodesigners had created a park-like environment, but the light was a constant reminder that the only thing protecting us from the full blast of the sun was a wall that was so thick and milky it diffused the small percentage of the sunlight that slipped past its molecules.

At that time—it was 2089, according to my records—the Mercury habitat was still something of a wonder. On the Moon, people still lived in stand-alone cities dug into the rims of craters. On Mars, they were still arguing about the rights and wrongs of full-scale terraforming. On Mercury, I could peer through the trees and observe the giant towers that supported a globe-circling greenhouse, three kilometers high and twenty kilometers wide. From space the habitat had looked like a thin white band that circled the planet at a sixty degree angle to the equator. Eventually, according to the developers, the urbs built into the towers were supposed to house a billion people.

"My drive wheel has developed structural defects," the car said. "I am instituting repair procedures."

Ling was the Elector's business manager—the factotum who took care of her employer's practical affairs, while the Elector concentrated on the creative efforts she considered the primary purpose of her life. Ling didn't miss a beat as she turned around in her chair and rested her finger on the car's main screen.

"Give us the details," Ling said.

The car had already slowed to a stop. "The drive wheel has developed three large cracks," the car reported. "Continued stress could result in collapse."

The Elector threw back her head. The electronic bracelets on her left arm flickered and rainbowed as she gestured at the landscape.

"I thought you told us this was a new vehicle, Joseph."

"How long will the repairs take?" Ling asked.

"Approximately ten minutes."

A small, single-passenger three-wheeler lurched off the road on our right and bumped across a tree root as it jockeyed past us. The transportation modes lining up behind our rear wheel included riding animals, two-passenger carts, and four hikers who were being followed by a motorized baggage hauler. The "road" was a narrow strip that was covered with a hard mat of surface grass. It had been designed so two vehicles going in opposite directions could just squeeze past each other.

By Mercury standards, the traffic on the road was uncomfortably dense. The high-speed vacuum rail had been shut down at the worst possible time. This section of the planet was approaching the beginning of its thousand-hour night. Half the people who lived in this part of the habitat had headed for the forest and a last-minute rendezvous with the pleasures of "outdoor life." Now all that recreational traffic had been inflated by the people who had decided to use the road net when the rail system had stopped operating.

Ling had jumped off the car and started examining the rear wheel. Her finger traced one of the cracks. She turned around and peered through the trees. She was wearing a close-fitting jacket-and-pants outfit, and her businesslike movements accented her slimness.

"My repair system has detected the presence of destructive molecular entities," the car said. "Remedial action is underway."

The Elector's bracelets shimmered again. "Is that thing telling us we're being *attacked*?"

Ling hopped back on the car and bent over the fabrication unit. She ran her hands across the unit's interface, and I realized she was searching its external databanks.

"I suppose we shouldn't be surprised," Ling said. "You were willing to come all the way to Mercury just to cast one vote. I suppose we shouldn't be surprised somebody might be willing to engage in a little violence just to stop one vote."

"A little violence!" the Elector orated. "Do you really consider this a *little* violence, Ling? Have you any idea what a clump of those things would have done if they'd landed on one of *us*?"

A red light flashed on top of the fabricator. The time strip on the side of the unit produced a 7:17 and held it.

"There's a car parked around that last bend," Ling said. "You can see it through the trees—right where they could have fired at us. I think there are four people in it."

"And once the repairs are made," I said, "they'll just follow us until they find another spot where they've got a good shot. And hold us up another ten minutes."

Ling gave me a quick glance of approval—the kind of glance that still evokes a foolish rush of pleasure, no matter how many times a woman who's captured my fancy bestows it on me.

"Are you telling me they merely have to stop us four times?" the Elector said.

Ling pointed at the time strip on the fabricator. "In seven minutes and seventeen seconds we can have our own version of the same kind of weapon they probably used—two minutes to download the fabrication program, five minutes and seventeen seconds to fabricate it. If you'll put your expense program on your notescreen, you can see just how much it will cost you, along with the price of half a dozen smoke bombs. The missiles we'll be firing should be the same type they're using—low impact devices equipped with moles that snip breaks in the long chain molecules that make up the plastic in the wheel. If Joe will give me some help when the time comes, I think we can arrange things so they have to sit around waiting for repairs while we put some distance between us."

The Elector wasn't really called the Elector. That was only a title I had bestowed on her in the privacy of my own mind. Her full name was Katrinka Yamioto Oldaf-Li, and the only thing she elected was the winners of a set of ten prizes. The prizes were awarded by an organization called the All-Mercury Coalition of Documented Creative Specialists, and they were presented to their proud recipients once every 88-day Mercury year.

The Elector was a well-known creator of the kind of simulated habitats the less-sophisticated members of the human community like to surround themselves with when they're forced to endure a few minutes of inactivity. (Not famous, please note—just well known. There's no reason you should feel culturally deficient if you've never encountered her name before.) I had sampled one of her creations during the voyage to Mercury, and it had been the kind of vision I tend to favor—an imaginary world in which people spent their lives dancing in elegant settings and browsing through gardens populated by citizens who dressed themselves with understated (but unmistakable) refinement. She liked clothes that flattered tall, slender men, but that was, from my viewpoint, the only serious flaw in her work.

Citizen Oldaf-Li had been living on Mercury when she had placed her first simulation on the market. She had spent most of the last ten years enjoying the pleasures of the Earth-orbiting cities, but she had maintained her membership in the All-Mercury Coalition of Documented Creative Specialists.

Now she was apparently one of the leaders in a faction that was trying to unseat the current officers. It was hard to believe anyone would spend three months in a spaceship for such a minor cause, but I had learned at a very early age that there were no limits to the absurdities humans would commit once they began joining organizations.

The gossips who follow my adventures on the databanks always make the same mistake when they compare me to Giacomo Casanova. They always focus on the number of women who burnished our days. They miss the deeper things we have in common. Casanova was born near the beginning of the 18th Century and I was born near the end of the 20th, but we would have given similar answers to certain questions if some time traveling psychologist had bedeviled us with the same personality assessment program. We would both have agreed that sexual encounters are a flat experience if they aren't combined with romantic feelings. We had both decided, at a very young age, that we would spend our lives following the impulses of our hearts. I had been seven years old the first time I had been awakened by the strange feelings a member of the other sex could evoke. I had been sixteen— and obsessively fascinated with a woman ten years older—when I had promised myself I would make those feelings the central concern of my life. I didn't want to waste one hour of my life listening to committee reports.

I had boarded the ship as the devoted companion of a flame-haired, amusing woman who was emigrating to Mercury to escape a burdensome grown son. I had believed we could keep each other diverted for the entire ninety-three days we were going to be imprisoned in the ship. Instead, I had discovered that I had exhausted her capacity for entertaining exchanges in the first five days of our liaison. On the forty-first day of the voyage—fifty-two days before we were scheduled to reach Mercury—I had placed my investments under the total control of my alter program and put myself into deep sleep.

And then, five minutes after I trudged through the disembarkation tunnel, while I was still feeling numb and semi-conscious—I turned my head as I maneuvered through the passenger lounge and saw Ling Chime sitting in front of a panoramic screen that displayed the craters and hard shadows of the real Mercury on the other side of the wall. She was sitting at a small, single-pedestal work table and staring at her notescreen as if she was planning a move in a championship game tournament.

The Elector had spent most of her time on the ship working at her trade. Ling had been less work oriented, but she had spent several hours each ship day superintending the Elector's business interests. I had seen her a few times during the first half of the voyage, and her face had always left me with an after-image that floated in my mind for several hours. But that had been all there had been to it.

So why had I responded with such a rush when I had seen Ling sitting in front of the panorama? Had it been the atmosphere created by the hard-shadowed desert behind her? Had it been the fact that she was focusing her entire attention on her notescreen and I was getting my first look at the intense competence she brought to everything she did?

I didn't know. I never would know. I just knew she had ignited the emotion that was, for me, the wine and the salt and the cream of life.

In Ling's case there was a small drawback—as there frequently is. I had picked up some information on Ling's background when I had been exploring the Elector's organizational antics. Ling had earned three doctorates and she still hadn't celebrated her thirty-second birthday.

The age entry had given me a mild shock. I can usually tell people's ages to within twenty years, no matter what they've done to keep their physiology and their appearance in peak condition. A woman of eighty and a woman of twenty-five may look almost exactly alike, but the older person will normally carry herself with an authority and sophistication that can't be simulated. I had watched Ling guide the Elector through one of the mandatory social rituals that had opened the voyage. She had been so self-possessed I had automatically assumed she was at least twice as old as she really was.

There had been a time when the discrepancy in ages wouldn't have troubled me. The older male, younger female pairing is a combination as old as the species. I didn't have any problem with the reverse situation either. When you're in your nineties, the fact that a woman is twenty years older than you doesn't make that much difference. But that was *my* attitude. It was already becoming obvious some of the younger members of our species were developing a different outlook.

I have been living with technological upheavals since I was old enough to regard the world with some measure of understanding. I was one of the first people to implant a musical performance system in my nervous system. I've struggled with the possibilities created by personality modification technology. I watched molecular technology flower into a major force after decades in which it looked like it was destined to be one of those tantalizing daydreams that remain permanently out of reach. Nothing, in my opinion, has changed the world more than the ability to modify human genes.

Moles have given us things like personal fabrication units and projects that could circle Mercury with a fully enclosed habitat in six Earth years. Genetic technology changed what we *are*. Ling could awe me with her competence because she had a brain and a nervous system that her parents had ordered for her in exactly the same way I had ordered my clothes. She could remain cool under stress because they had chosen a set of glands that equipped her with that kind of temperament.

So why was someone like Ling working as a personal assistant to someone like the Elector? What did she think when she looked at someone like *me*? Was I just a primitive life form to her? An old man fumbling around the Solar System with an outmoded set of physical components?

The woman who had drawn me to Mercury had been fleeing a son who was six years younger than Ling. Her son apparently believed men and women my age were the ultimate enemy—a group that was going to sit on society and block every channel of advancement for centuries into the future. *I gave him everything I could*, his mother had said. *A forty percent intelligence enhancement. Looks. A coordination component that would have made him a professional athlete when you and I were young. Aggressiveness. And what do I get? A son who tells me I'm as obsolete as a piece of thirty-year-old software.*

The Elector started gesturing and emoting as soon as she realized I was steering myself across the lounge toward Ling's work table. It didn't take me long to find out why Ling was working with such intensity. The Elector had planned to hop out of the orbit-to-surface shuttle and board one of the high-speed rail vehicles that raced through the vacuum just outside the habitat. She would arrive, according to her calculations, three hours before the deadline for casting her vote. Unfortunately, the governing body of Mercury—the Conclave of Talents—had once again decided it had to worry about the safety and long-term well-being of the people it was supposed to serve. The Talents had decided this section of the rail system needed some special maintenance work. It would be six hours before a vehicle glided down the rails.

Ling was looking for a road vehicle the Elector could buy or rent. If she could find one sometime in the next half hour, they could drive past four stations and board a functioning rail vehicle. I watched Ling work at her notescreen while the Elector paced out big circles behind us. Then I slipped away to another table and opened my own notescreen.

My financial program updated its statement on my current worth, and I asked it for a list of the current bids for road vehicles. The top bid on the list had been posted by Ling, and it had been totally ignored. As I had expected, most of the people who already owned road vehicles weren't interested in selling.

I stared at the figures on my screen. If I doubled Ling's offer, I would be eating up almost twenty-five percent of the profits my alter had earned for me while I had been asleep....

Most of the immediate responses came from idlers who apparently thought I was some kind of ignorant off-worlder. Five people advised me I could turn right as I left the disembarkation lounge and find a shop with a large-scale fabrication unit that could produce any vehicle I wanted within five hours.

In case you haven't noticed, one wit expounded, *you're living in a society in which you can have anything you want for the price of a little energy, some cheap raw materials, and a small payment to the people who designed the product and wrote the fabrication program. I realize you've just landed on our planet. But we have more of the civilized conveniences than you may think.*

I said I need it immediately, I replied. *IMMEDIATELY.*

It was a reckless thing to do—an invitation to squeeze me until I strangled. But it brought results. An image of a three-wheeler bounced onto my screen seconds after I finished writing. The list of accessories indicated the owner had been planning a romantic trip of her own. The asking price was thirty percent higher than the amount I had offered.

Ling was still hunting down possibilities when I hurried back to her table. "Please excuse me for interfering in your problems," I said. "I have just been reassessing my own plans. As it happens, I ordered a touring road vehicle before we left Earth. If you would be willing to share my accommodations for the next few hours...."

Ling pulled two sections of a weapon out of the fabrication unit and fitted them together. Her new possession was a practical-looking device with a skinny barrel and a wide, bulky stock.

"There are five smoke bombs in the fabricator, Joe. Can you drop two of them over the side when I give the word? Then tell the car to move. And drop more bombs as you roll."

"I don't think that will put too much stress on my martial capabilities."

"What makes you think they won't fire through the smoke?" the Elector demanded. "They'll still know exactly where we are."

"I'm assuming they're not trying to kill us," Ling said. "They can't fire through the smoke without running the risk they'll hit one of us."

I watched her as she slipped around the front wheels and started working her way through the trees. Fashion was once again going through a period in which clothes and body styles emphasized the classic sexual differentiators. Women were spotlighting their breasts, wearing long skirts, and even draping themselves in the kind of elaborate gowns the Elector favored. Men were developing their shoulder muscles and adopting clothes that drew attention to the results.

It was a development I could support with enthusiasm. What was the point in having two sexes if there wasn't any difference between them? I was too short to look physically impressive, but I had grown a beard and put myself through a training program that made me look solid and muscular. Ling had managed to conform to fashion without compromising her ability to function. She had picked clothes that emphasized her litheness and the gracefulness of her movements. Her hair had been cut so it bobbed just above her shoulders.

There have been times—many times, unfortunately—when people have looked at the woman who had currently aroused my interest and wondered why she had paired off with someone like me. In this case, I honestly thought we would make an attractive couple. If I could lure Ling away from her employer for a few tendays, we could enjoy an interlude that would be a nice mix of companionship and sensuality. We could follow the temperate zone, perhaps, as it moved around the planet. Or would Ling prefer the kind of long twilight we were currently experiencing?

"Don't you think it might be best if you didn't stare at her?" the Elector said. "Even if they didn't see her leave the car, they might wonder why you're so fixated on that part of the landscape."

I stood up and glanced into the fabricator. Five oval objects had been lined up on a storage shelf.

The car's main screen emitted a trio of discrete trumpet notes. *There's a red activation button on the side of each bomb*, a written message from Ling announced. *You can release the bombs whenever the car tells you the wheel's repaired.*

I examined one of the bombs without pulling it out of the fabricator. The Elector was eyeing me with an ironic smile.

"You have intriguing tastes, Joseph Louis. I have to confess I thought *I* was the one you were interested in."

I shrugged. "My reactions to women are totally unpredictable. I thought about having them modified many years ago. But I decided I'd rather just let them lead me where they will."

"And that's why you've led such an adventurous life?"

"Believe me, it's been much less turbulent than the entries in the databanks indicate. Most of the time, it's just a matter of a few hours with this one, or a few tendays with that one. I'm interested in pleasure, not excitement."

"And how much time are you planning to spend with Ling? I should warn you—we're heading back to civilization ninety-eight hours after I cast my vote."

I stared at her. "You're going to turn right around and pen yourself up in a spaceship for another three months?"

"I can do my kind of work wherever I am. I'm far happier, in fact, when I'm someplace where I don't have to put up with *weather*. I moved into this place two years after it opened and I got tired of hearing people lecture me about it before I'd been here a single Mercury year. Every time we had a rain storm I had to listen to somebody telling me I should be happy I was living in an environment that was so big it could maintain its own cycles *just like the Earth does*. Personally, I'd rather pay the extra rent and live in environments that have to be managed down to the last molecule of air."

"The repairs have been completed," the car said. "I await your orders."

I turned away from her before she could see the gloom that was settling over my face. My hands ripped two bombs out of the fabricator and dropped them onto the road surface. Two red clouds enveloped the car.

I watched the clouds expand along the road. We had been traveling toward the night side of the planet, so the wind inside the habitat was actually blowing in the direction we had been moving. The temperature difference between the night side and the day side could have built up enormous winds inside the habitat, but the engineers had arranged things so the air flow remained mild and steady. The habitat had been designed with several doglegs, and the landscaping had included hills that could act as windbreaks. The trees probably helped, too.

I ordered the car to resume progress, and we edged forward. Puzzled faces stared at me through the fog as two three-wheelers passed us going in the other direction.

The smoke had covered the entire width of the road behind me. I looked back and saw Ling skimming through the mist with the long strides of the expert low-gravity runner. I had spent several tendays mastering that skill when I had first emigrated to the Moon. I wasn't surprised to discover I would never do it as well as she could.

The face on the Elector's notescreen belonged to a man who had adopted a particularly masculine style: a large, bald head and a trim, disciplined beard. I had come across several vindictive graphics when I had been browsing through the Elector's political diatribes. I immediately knew I was looking at the current Elected Superintendent of the All-Mercury Coalition of Documented Creative Specialists.

I had spent several hours exploring two of the Elected Superintendent's environments during the voyage. I wouldn't have paid much attention to them normally, but they had been well crafted, and they certainly kept my activity hormones flowing. The Superintendent created fantasy worlds for people who wanted to combat various kinds of imaginary opponents and dispatch various kinds of imaginary animals. In person, he was scrupulously polite. It was the Elector who launched into a tirade ten words after she heard his perfectly modulated greeting.

As I understood it, the officers represented a group that wanted to alter the membership rules of the Coalition. Under the current membership rules, voting members had to produce a certain number of creative works every twenty-five Mercury years. The officers wanted to increase the requirements. They had already managed to limit voting on certain issues to people who were actually physically present on Mercury. They had even decreed that voting members had to establish their right to vote by attending a meeting or paying a personal visit to the elections officer at least once every seven Eyears.

As far as I could determine, the Coalition had only one function: it awarded the All-Mercury prizes for the "finest, most innovative works produced on the First Planet" during the shortest year the laws of physics had bestowed on any rock in the Solar System. The right to vote on the awards seemed to be the sole benefit of membership.

The members of the Elector's faction felt larger principles were involved. As they saw it, their group favored a "broadbased, fully representative" organization that would admit "anyone who had been gifted with the true creative fire." The Superintendent's group was "a ring of audience-pandering would-be oligarchs" determined to "garrote creative minds who have already been asphyxiated by the abuse-by-neglect they have received from the semi-conscious commercial audience."

The Elector didn't quite use language like that. She had too much taste. But the attack on our car had confirmed her belief that the Superintendent was a violent man who catered to the worst human impulses. The Superintendent maintained an expression of calm concern as he stared at her while she ranted.

"Do you really feel we should be wasting time rehashing our differences, Katrinka? It seems to me you should call the police."

"You know very well that if we call the police they'll merely get us involved in a lot of time-consuming questioning. *We are going to arrive on time. I am going to cast my vote.*"

"I hope you will. I wish all our members took their voting privileges as seriously as you do."

"*Voting is not a privilege!* Voting is a *right*. The mere fact that you call it a privilege should tell anyone who cares about social justice everything they need to know."

We had reached the edge of a long, narrow lake while the Elector had been venting her emotions. Ten minutes earlier I might have thought the lake created a picturesque scene. Now, the water looked dark and cold. The complicated shadows the trees cast on the surface looked as sinister as a tract of quicksand.

How could anyone turn around, a third of a tenday after they had made landfall, and go back to the jail cells we had been living in since we had left the Earth-Moon system?

I turned back to the Elector. "Wouldn't you be better off talking to some of the people on your side? It seems to me they could use an attack like this as a propaganda ploy."

Ling gave me another example of those golden looks of approval. I was obviously saying something she had wanted to say herself.

The Elector banished the Superintendent from her notescreen with a wave of her hand—a gesture that would have looked appallingly rude if I hadn't been confident he was probably happy to have the conversation terminated.

"By this time," the Elector said, "everyone who's going to vote has undoubtedly voted."

"Then why bother to vote yourself? Do you really think there's any serious possibility your side could lose by one vote?"

"Ling, will you take manual control of this vehicle and see if you can achieve a little more speed than this parade line we're in is making? If it wouldn't be too much trouble."

Ling settled behind the main control screen. She stared at the menus for approximately twenty seconds—I'm certain it couldn't have been longer—and we swerved out of line and passed four of the vehicles in front of us.

The Elector returned her attention to the semi-intelligent wretch who had questioned the value of her activities. "There are important principles at issue here, Joseph. Some of us feel there is more to life than the pursuit of pleasure."

"You're going to spend a total of six months in a spaceship," I said, "with just half a tenday in a place where you can actually walk around like a human being—"

"No one should object to a minor hardship when they're defending a major cause. It may even help Ling develop a little toughness—she's still getting her first look at the universe, after all."

The Elector eyed me over a mocking smile. She really was an unusual woman. She really believed she was doing something moral and laudable. Yet at the same time she couldn't resist reminding me I was pursuing someone who had been born just after I reached my sixties.

The Elector's smile changed to a look of pure annoyance. I started to respond, and then realized she was staring at something in front of our vehicle.

I turned around and discovered I was regarding the hindquarters of a large gray animal. I had never seen a reduced-scale riding elephant before, but I was familiar with the concept. This one was a little taller than a horse. Its rider was lounging on a top mounted arrangement that looked like a luxury-class acceleration couch.

Ling had tried to move us over to the left, to pass the animal, but it was straddling the center of the road. The elephant's passenger had his hands behind his head and he was lolling back with his chest bared and his eyes on the sky—as if he thought the milky whiteness above the trees could bestow some kind of life-giving radiation on his skin.

He wasn't quite as oblivious of the scene around him as he pretended. He moved to the right, as if he was giving us room, but as soon as he did it we saw there was a car coming toward us in the other lane. As soon as the car passed, the elephant shifted back toward the center.

If he had stopped dead, we could have driven off the road and slipped by him. The Conclave of Talents had established certain rules for vehicles using their roads, and they had embedded their dictates in every vehicle's programming. You couldn't exceed forty kilometers an hour and you couldn't drive off the road unless it was blocked by a stationary object.

There were good reasons for such rules. The forest was the source of all the oxygen and organic raw materials available in the habitat. The roads in the forest weren't supposed to be used for routine travel. They had been added to the forest area so people could reach pleasure spots in comfort.

The Talents had shut down part of the rail system because they felt it needed maintenance. They forced cars to stay on the road because they were worried about the maintenance of the habitat's biological life support system. Their obsession with maintenance was a nuisance at the moment, but it would have irritated me more when I had been a self-centered scatterbrain in my twenties and thirties. Overall, it was a good argument for the Mercurian's experiment with a "democracy of limited choice." The Talents had divided into factions and parties, like any other group of politicians, but there were areas in which they had reached an almost unshakeable consensus. They had all noted that human societies tend to neglect the long-term maintenance of the ecosystems and technological infrastructures that support their way of life.

Ling had already collected a good view of the elephant rider's face and queried the external databanks. My notescreen networked her results, and I skimmed through a search summary that advised me the gentleman on the elephant belonged to an extended family of medical designers. The Yan family had built up one of the most successful enterprises on Mercury. They were quartered in a tower just north of us, and they made most of their profits designing replacement parts and enhancements.

"Do you mind if I talk to him?" I said. "He seems to have connections—a little diplomacy might be prudent."

"We've already lost enough time dealing with the terrorists our hoodlum friends sent after us," the Elector said. "Do you really feel we should sit here trying to argue with this oaf while they get back in range?"

I leaned over the front of the car and addressed the oaf in my most polished Techno-Mandarin. He gave me the benefit of two or three glances while I entreated with him, but apparently he wasn't in the mood to engage in actual conversation.

There had been a few shouts from the cars behind us when he had started playing his little game, but I noticed they had all died down. By now, most of our fellow pilgrims would have had him identified. Apparently, they didn't feel inclined to argue with him.

He looked like a type I had encountered more than once. Those of us who live on the fringes of conventional society tend to run into them. According to the data on my notescreen, his name was Yan Daian and he was the son of one of the more prominent women in his clan. He had been born in 2031—when I had still been ricocheting through my thirties—and he listed his occupation as "lifestyle consultant." He was, in other words, someone who was enjoying an extended adolescence, thanks to the income and social status he acquired from his family connections.

I turned back to the Elector. "Isn't there some kind of law against this kind of behavior?"

"There are certain things our beloved Talents seem to feel we should settle among ourselves. They'll hobble us with a thousand rules designed to protect us from our fondness for so-called short-term thinking and refuse to intervene when someone creates a situation they consider a minor inconvenience. They claim they're trying to minimize wasteful legal tangles."

"Maybe we should give him a few minutes of privacy. It's been my experience people like him tend to get tired of their games pretty quickly."

The Elector was standing by the fabricator. She glanced at the time strip, and I realized it was ticking off the last seconds of a countdown.

"The Talents think we should deal with these problems on our own, Joseph."

She plunged her hands into the fabricator. Her right arm stretched above her head. A round object arced over the front of our vehicle.

I turned around and saw a thin mist rising from the road surface. The elephant's body sagged as if all that mass of bone and muscle had been transformed into a pile of gray cloth. Its passenger rolled off his seat as his mount settled to the ground.

"Move!" the Elector shouted. "Drive off the road."

Under the rules, we could now leave the road and circle the inanimate object blocking our progress. Unfortunately, the Elector had forgotten the object's cargo might have other ideas.

Yan Daian came out of his roll and crossed the road in a perfectly calculated low-gravity jump. He skimmed over the top of his recumbent animal and landed just in front of us, with his arms waving. His face twisted into a mask of outrage. I had realized he was tall and bony when I had seen him reclining on the elephant, but now I could see just how exaggerated his physique was. His height was all in his legs—as if his upper body was mounted on stilts. His legs were at least twenty percent longer than they should have been, given the length of his torso.

The three-wheeler's programming overrode Ling's commands and we eased to a stop. The object dancing in front of us was undeniably mobile.

Ling's face settled into the same focused, businesslike look it had assumed when she had set off through the woods with the gun. She stood up and covered the distance between her and the fabricator in two deliberate, unhurried steps.

Yan Daian was obviously furious, but he wasn't trying to communicate his emotions with words. He was just dancing in front of us, deliberately manipulating the programming that was fixing us in place. The Elector was the one who was making all the noise.

The more I watched that silent figure gyrate, the less I liked the situation. I turned my back on him and stepped up to Ling. "He's not making threats," I murmured. "No threats. No insults. That's not a good sign when somebody has the kind of family he seems to have."

The light on the fabricator interface turned green. Ling reached inside and pulled out a couple of dozen objects that were about the size of her little finger.

"If he's called for help," Ling said, "they're already on the way."

She dropped out of the three-wheeler and I decided to follow her. This wasn't the first time I had watched people fling non-lethal weapons at their adversaries. It's been my experience that non-lethals are the kind of technological marvels that usually work better when they're supported by more primitive techniques.

She stopped to give Yan Daian a warning—the first foolish thing I had seen her do. "These things are quite painful. Worse than animal bites or electric shocks. They cling to your skin and inject moles that stimulate your pain receptors. Please don't make me use them. We're not interested in causing you or your animal the slightest discomfort."

Naturally, he lunged at her before she'd finished delivering her speech. He bent over and tucked himself in, but some of the weapons in her first handful landed on bare skin anyway.

He straightened up as soon as the pain jolted him. His head snapped back. He lurched away from her and hopped around in front of the car with his arms waving and his mouth warped into a silent scream.

Ling tossed a second handful at his chest, but it didn't change the situation.

"You should have used a gas," the Elector shouted. "You should have knocked him out."

I'm not a violent person, but I had become tougher as I had aged. Technology had helped me overcome some of my reluctance, too. There's very little you can do to people nowadays that can't be repaired in a few hours. I had severed my spinal cord in a motorcycle accident in my youth and been forced to spend four tendays in the hospital—two of them in almost absolute immobility. Today, I believe that problem can be dealt with in six Edays.

I approached Yan Daian from the rear and launched two carefully placed kicks. He went down with both his ankles broken, and I grabbed his legs and pulled him off the road.

Ling stared at me for a moment. Then she reached into the three-wheeler and pulled out the weapon she had used to slow down our pursuers.

"Hop on board and start rolling," Ling said. "I'll take care of the Superintendent's friends. They should be pulling up the road in a couple of minutes."

"And what about the over-age adolescent over there? What are you going to do when his reinforcements arrive?"

"Get in the car, Joe. Please."

I looked up at the Elector. "Go ahead without me. Don't waste time."

The Elector looked a little stunned, but she really was dominated by her political passions. She gave the three-wheeler an order, and it lurched off the road and bypassed the unconscious elephant. On the other side of the road, Yan Daian was grunting with pain as he dictated something into his notescreen.

I smiled at Ling. "It will be an adventure," I said. "Besides, you'll never meet anybody who's had more experience at running away. Have you ever been pursued by three angry husbands simultaneously?"

She walked away from me and dropped to one knee beside a tree. I had never seen anyone who had more control over her responses. I have spent a large part of my life learning to interpret the information communicated by things like the slant of a woman's shoulders and the subtle changes that cross her face. Ling was giving me nothing. I could have been talking to a computer screen.

I've always responded to faces that communicate something. It could be almost any desirable quality—tenderness, intelligence, enthusiasm, serenity. But it had to be *something*. Why was I fascinated by a face that told me nothing?

I could only assume it had something to do with her incredible air of absolute competence. I have watched women climb mountains. I have seen hundreds of women play musical instruments. I have even observed surgeons who worked on eyes and nervous systems. There is nothing more beautiful than a woman who combines competence with all the physical and temperamental qualities that evoke romantic and sensual feelings—assuming, of course, that you're the kind of person who tends to have such feelings.

I selected a position behind another tree and put a map of my immediate area on my notescreen. One thing you should look for when you're making a getaway is a crowd. I didn't expect to encounter a real crowd in a forest, but I located something almost as good. Just south of us, approximately three thousand people were participating in some kind of woodland festival.

There was a short description of the festival linked to the map. They were hunting a unicorn, of all things. The animal had been released just a few standard hours before, and they were driving it toward the sunward side of the habitat. Eventually they would pin it against the sunward wall. A cage would be lowered over it. Wine drinking and other activities would celebrate the triumph.

The tower that housed the Yan family was located about twenty kilometers from our current location. They couldn't reach us without detouring around the lake that stretched between us and them. With a little luck, we should be able to reach the edges of the festival before the Yan's emissaries caught up with us.

Ling raised her weapon and pulled the trigger in a single, uninterrupted motion. She was standing up and flowing into a run almost as soon as the gun emitted its last, almost inaudible, phut.

I fell in beside her and told her what I'd found. "We'll probably have to engage in some informal sexual activity," I said. "It's not normally my kind of thing, but my impression is it won't be too bad. The whole affair has a kind of light-hearted air. I don't know what you've learned about me from the databanks, but what I really like is a total emotional experience with someone I find genuinely attractive."

"And you're going to all this trouble because you think you can have that kind of experience with *me*?"

Normally, I'm happier when things just develop. You put yourself in the right position and let things happen. But you also have to remember you aren't in complete control of the schedule. The great truth about sexual relationships—the difficulty that makes them endlessly fascinating—is the fact that they involve two people.

It wasn't the best moment. I had been living in low-gravity environments for almost twenty years, but I still had to concentrate when I ran. The designers had broken up the forest floor with shrubbery. Some of the trees they had developed had big, spreading roots.

"I've been hoping it might be a possibility," I said.

I must have covered twenty more steps before I realized she wasn't going to respond. It was one of those moments when my emotions let me know just how strong they really are. I try to treat the whole thing lightly—there is no danger, after all, that I'm going to die or be permanently maimed if one of my adventures doesn't turn out. I'm merely going to miss an experience that's aroused a yearning. But it doesn't feel that way when I find myself faced with the kind of reaction her silence seemed to be communicating.

I wanted *her*. Don't tell me I'll want someone else in another tenday. I haven't seen that someone else yet.

I looked down at her feet and tried to convince myself the situation couldn't be completely hopeless. She was still matching me stride for stride. She could have been moving at least thirty percent faster if she had decided to speed up and leave me behind.

"There's something I think I should tell you," Ling said. "My sexual appetites aren't very strong. They're almost as weak as you can get them and still have any. The emotional side of my sexual feelings is just as weak. I still respond to the other sex emotionally. But it's nothing like the kind of overwhelming obsession you seem to experience. My mother thought that was the best way to be."

"And you're happy that way? You haven't thought you might like to strengthen your feelings?"

"It's the way I am. Are you happy with the way you are?"

"I'm not sure happiness is relevant. To me, it's like being immersed in music. I'm surrounded by creatures who seem beautiful and exciting."

I turned my head away from her and decided I might as well concentrate on our immediate problem. "I've had another thought that might be useful," I said. "Why don't we see if we can enlist some help from the quartet who've been pursuing us on the road? Katrinka's obviously going to cast her vote. The Superintendent's faction may be certain they're going to win the election, but she can still raise a fuss about the tactics they used. If they gave us some help now—in exchange for some silence on Katrinka's part...."

"Do you really think they might think that way?"

"I just wondered if you thought it was worth a try."

"I haven't got the slightest idea. The people who shot at our wheel may not even be members of the Coalition. The Superintendent has a lot of friends who are interested in weapons and military techniques. Katrinka likes to refer to them as his hoodlum associates."

"You think they might have attacked us just because they were friends of his?"

"I don't know. I really can't tell you what any of these people are feeling, Joe. I've just been doing my job."

The Superintendent appeared on my notescreen as soon as the program advised me it had placed the call. I filled him in as rapidly as I could, in my best impersonation of a direct, no-nonsense, business-oriented male.

"What are you trying to do?" he asked. "Arrange a romp with Lady Compassion?"

"As a matter of fact, no. I'm just trying to see if Ling and I can get out of this mess without sustaining any serious damage."

"You've paired off with her assistant? This is the first time anyone on her side has done something I can understand."

"I'm not on her side. I haven't participated in a political controversy since I was a teenager."

"You helped her out, didn't you? You crippled a member of the Yan family just so she could continue her grand journey to the polling site. You do understand what kind of people the Yans are? You didn't do something like that without consulting the databanks?"

"I merely offered Katrinka the kind of assistance any—"

"Quit while you're ahead. I've cued in my friends while we were talking. They'll love every minute of it."

We had reached the edge of the festival. I could see two groups making their way through the trees. One group had spread out in a thin line and seemed to be maintaining a fairly serious level of alertness. The members of the other group seemed to be more interested in the bottles they were carrying and the bodies they were grasping.

I had been wearing a green jacket with some distinctive gold striping woven into the lower sleeves. I draped it over my arm, with the sleeves tucked inside, and told Ling she should throw her own jacket over her shoulders—a move that broke up her rather distinctive outline. Her gun went into a thick patch of vines. She had ordered a use-and-recycle version. There was no way we could break it down and conceal it under her jacket.

"It's probably just as well," I said. "We've already inflicted more damage on the Yan family than anyone in his senses should have. None of these little changes are going to give us any permanent protection, but they can give us some hope we won't be identified the instant we're eyeballed by somebody who's been given our description. Now if we can put a little distance between us, so we don't look like a couple.…"

I gave our position to the Superintendent's friends, and headed for the group that seemed to be more pleasure oriented. In a moment, Ling was ensconced between two men who were clutching at her waist and her shoulders. She looked up at the man on her left, and I saw her smile for the first time.

An arm slipped around my shoulder and pressed my head against a female breast. I raised my eyes and discovered I had fallen into the clutches of a woman who was at least two heads taller than I am.

I marched through the woods with my hands grasping at human flesh, struggling to keep track of Ling in spite of the fascinating swells and indentations that intruded on my field of vision. I was so busy playing my role that I almost didn't react when I saw two long-legged figures flitting through the woods. They were using a low-gravity technique that maximized the value of their leg length. They were taking deliberate, ultra-long steps and carefully making sure they didn't leave the ground and waste time coming down. It was a very efficient way to move in low gravity—if you didn't mind a physique that made you look like some of your ancestors had been water-skimming insects.

Ling had already started pulling her two companions toward a patch of waist-high grass that had accumulated around a small pond. Her body was sinking downward in a way that made it obvious what she had in mind.

The two longlegs stared at me and took two steps in my direction. My partner tried to hold onto me as I slipped away from her, but my exercise program had given me some useful extra muscle mass.

I pulled out my notescreen and gave the Superintendent's rowdies another fix on my position as I started accelerating. I had been assuming the Superintendent was one of those baronial males who feel they have to keep their word. Now I was beginning to wonder if he might be the type who went in for cruel jokes.

The two longlegs looked like they were picking their way across a pond, rock by rock, but I knew I would be misjudging the whole situation if I thought I could outrun them. My only hope was the possibility my reinforcements really were on their way.

I spotted them before I had managed to cover a hundred meters. They were actually wearing the kind of costumes Europeans wore when they traipsed through the African parks when I was young.

I waved at them frantically, and they halted and gestured at me to join them. I threw a glance over my shoulder and discovered two sets of oversize legs were tiptoeing toward me on my left rear, with about fifty meters between us.

You have two choices in a situation like that. You can give up, or you can torment yourself and prolong the chase. I usually decide to torment myself.

I veered toward a promising tree and jumped at the lowest branch. I had been living on the Moon for the last few years, so the gravity on Mercury was actually stronger than the gravity field my muscles were used to. I managed to get a grip on the branch anyway. I even hauled myself upright and worked my way onto the branch above it.

The longlegs stopped under the tree. For a moment I thought they might be content just to tree me while they requested instructions. I could see one of them talking into his notescreen as I put another layer of branches between me and the base of the tree. Then the other one bent at the knees, and I watched him float off the ground. He rolled onto his side and eased himself onto the branch I had just vacated.

He was mostly legs, but his arms had received some genetic assistance, too. It was obviously time I switched from flight to fight. I did, after all, have the advantage that I commanded the high ground.

We played a few moves of a little game: he ran around on the lower branches, looking for an opportunity to get up to my level, and I maneuvered so I would always be in a good position to stomp on his hands as soon as he got near me.

The game ended when his partner folded up the notescreen and prepared to join the fun. On the ground, my four bodyguards were still acting like they would be happy to perform all kinds of derring-do if I would just cross the distance between us and link up with their group.

Ling had covered at least three steps before I realized she had broken out of the grassy area in which she had been engaging in pleasanter recreational activities. The second waterbug had elevated himself to the first branch, and I was trying to watch both of them at the same time. Ling was flying toward the Superintendent's friends as if she had been launched from a catapult.

I didn't see her grab their gun. I was watching my adversaries maneuver into a good position for a pincer attack. They were talking very conversationally—like people who knew exactly what they were doing and believed I couldn't do anything in response if I heard them coordinating their efforts. Then the one on the right snapped back his head and produced a noise that sounded like a cross between a scream and a gargle. The other one joined him in the chorus, and I watched them clutch at the branches with both arms as they tried to maintain their hold on the tree.

The Superintendent's henchmen were willing to drive us back to the tower near the spaceport, but they rolled off as soon as we climbed out of their three-wheeler. They had already called the Yan family and apologized for the fact that missiles from their gun had left two Yan employees sitting under a tree with broken legs. The Superintendent had apparently overestimated their zest for conflict with people who took it seriously.

"I'll give you my best assessment of the situation," one of them had told me. "You won't like it, but it's the best advice anyone can give you, colleague. Try to hole up until you can leave Mercury. There aren't many places where you can hide from the Yan family for long. Their theory of human relations is dominated by one big principle—their neighbors should be afraid of them. But you might pull it off."

The spaceport tower was an obvious choice, but it housed two of the biggest hotels on the planet. I had already reserved a suite equipped with the optimum security package.

It was a nice little fortress. The walls were meter-thick active defense units. The electronic systems were monitored by detection routines that would switch everything to a new path if they spotted an anomaly that lasted a hundredth of a second. The food and wine programs in the fabricator were as select as the programs in the three-wheeler I had rented. The besieged could eat and drink like potentates without opening a single chink in their defenses.

Ling raised her eyebrows when she tasted the first bottle I opened after we secured the one and only door.

"In answer to your question," I said, "I can pay the bill for this right up to the day your ship leaves. Unfortunately, at that point I won't be able to buy a passage on the ship for myself."

"This is way out of my orbit financially, Joe. You shouldn't expect any significant help from Katrinka, either. She'll just tell herself you did all this because of me."

I raised my glass. "We're free and we're secure. And one of us is supposed to be incredibly bright."

"So what do you want me to do? Plug into your financial alter and see if I can snatch up a few million yuris?"

I shook my head. "At this point, I don't think the best human brain in the Solar System could *follow* the things my alter does."

"You have two problems if we stay in this suite until the next ship leaves for Earth-Luna. First, you need to raise the money for your own ticket. Then, you have to get from here to the orbiter without being captured."

"And what do you suggest I do about them?"

"I presume your alter has a risk setting. Set it as high as you're willing to set it. You may lose everything—but at this point you really don't have anything to lose. For the escape to the orbiter—I'll work out a tactical plan and see what kind of weapons we'll need."

She said it very coolly, of course—just as coolly as she had assessed the situation and gone into action when we had been attacked on the road.

For the last twenty years, my alter had been operating with the risk factor set at twenty-three percent. It couldn't venture into a situation unless it was certain I wouldn't lose more than twenty-three percent of my capital. I wasn't trying to get rich. I was just trying to maximize my life style without engaging in that restrictive, time-wasting activity called work.

"I would call that a fallback plan," I said. "We've got a lot of things we can work with. We're operating on a world with a population of approximately five hundred million people. The Yans have to have political adversaries. There should be some divisions in the Conclave we can work on, too. The Talents can't be one hundred percent in favor of this hands-off policy. They're still people, no matter what they've done to themselves."

"I don't know anything about politics. I just gave you my best advice. I gave up trying to understand politics when I was a teenager. I'm an administrator—I work with accounting programs, I schedule Katrinka's trips, I make sure her customers get what they want. I think you got the wrong impression when you saw me reacting when our wheel got hit. I'm not some kind of supergenius strategist."

I spoke American English when I was young. We had a word in those days that described people who were very good at things like math and science, but didn't know a thing about human relationships, and didn't seem to have much interest in the activities most people found pleasurable. It was a derogatory word with a derogatory sound—nerd. They don't seem to have developed an equivalent word in the off-Earth societies—perhaps because their cultures have too much respect for learning and technical expertise.

It had taken me awhile to learn there was such a thing as a beautiful female nerd, but it had been a useful discovery. At least a third of the scientists I had been in love with would have been considered prime specimens when the term had been in vogue. They could have spent their whole lives in their laboratories and field camps and never felt they were missing anything important. Nerdhood wasn't as obvious when a woman could dazzle you with her looks, of course. You don't need social skills when half the humans you encounter are males who think you're doing them a big favor if you just stand still while they try to entertain you.

Ling had doctorates in cosmology, administrative organization, and number theory. They are all fascinating subjects. I'm certain there were times when they made her heart thump with excitement. But you could master everything the human race knew about all three of them without spending one moment wondering if another human being was going to do something you wanted them to do.

"And you're happy spending your life helping someone like Katrinka?" I said.

She shrugged. "It's easy work. It leaves me plenty of time to pay attention to other things."

She smiled. It was a shy, guarded smile, but at that moment, in spite of everything, it glittered as if somebody had been shining a spotlight on her.

"I'm still deciding what I want to do with my life, Joe. That's one of the differences between people in your age cohort and people my age. When you were young, you didn't know you could have centuries ahead of you."

"And right now you feel you're only good at planning financial programs and shoot 'em ups?"

"I'm a member of three circles that are looking at different approaches to the open universe question. I'm part of the outer circle of two groups that are looking at mathematical issues most mathematicians have never heard of. But don't ask me to help you manipulate political systems. For that you have to understand the emotions of the people involved. You have to feel the same things they feel."

"Someone who can be happy working for Katrinka," I said, "obviously doesn't know much about feelings like vanity and the drive for social status."

"Is that a flaw? Does it change your feelings about me?"

"Right now—at this moment—you are the most desirable woman in the Solar System."

Her shoulders relaxed just a little—just enough that I could see it. Her eyes turned inward.

"Does that matter to you?" I said.

"Right now—at this moment… yes."

Her responses were gentle, as you would expect. But they were real. We could spend a very pleasant time together, if we ever got our troubles straightened out.

When I had left Earth in 2071, I had been approached by a representative from an agency that engaged in an activity it called "preventive peacekeeping." She had noticed that I had bounced around the home planet like a billiard ball and become enmeshed in the social structures of most of the places I visited. She hadn't asked me to *spy*. She had merely offered me a small guaranteed stipend in return for reports and observations.

When she had learned I was embarking for Mercury, she had given me some contacts who could help me pursue my social rounds. The Mercurian political system was a novel idea at the time. Her agency wanted to make sure I got a good look at it.

I left Ling sleeping on the bed and asked my notescreen for a complete list of all the members of the Conclave of Talents, with their official personality profiles. The Mercurian constitution writers hadn't been able to agree on a single personality type. The whole scheme had almost failed when their constitutional convention had been split between the people who favored moral virtues like compassion and the people who favored intellectual qualities like the ability to absorb huge amounts of information.

In the end, they had compromised. Citizens who wanted to join the official candidate pool had their choice of four different personality clusters. Pick the one you could live with, schedule a few sessions with a certified, state of the art personality modification program, and you, too, could spend your life groveling for votes and debating the best design for the latest upgrade to the recycling system.

I thought it was a promising idea the first time I heard of it, and I still think it's probably one of the better political systems humans have cobbled together. The basic trouble with all political systems is the material they work with: the human personality. If you tell the voters they can only elect people who possess certain personality traits, you're going to eliminate most of the afflictions that have plagued democracies since the Greeks first started experimenting with the idea.

You could go further, of course. You could modify the personalities of the *voters*. But that would mean *I* would have to change.

At the moment, the Conclave of Talents seemed to be dominated by people with two kinds of personality clusters: the Bos and the Mings. The other two clusters—the Joos and the Xins—only held about twenty-five percent of the seats in the Conclave.

In spite of that, I felt I would have better luck if I appealed to a Xin. For one thing, most Xins were women.

If I had been on Mercury longer, I would have had a detailed picture of the political situation in my head. As it was, I had to spend three hours rummaging through the databanks just so I could piece together a rudimentary cartoon. Ling was standing behind me by the time I was done. She sat down beside me, and I studied the information on the screen while we mixed the aroma of coffee with the flavors of lobster and sausage pastries.

"The Xins are an interesting cluster," I said. "Apparently there was a faction who felt they needed some politicians who were adventurous and novelty seeking. So they compromised and balanced the adventurousness with an intense need for community approval."

I called up a three-dimensional diagram of the social and political alignments that influenced the Talent pool. It was mostly based on numbers and links I had worked out myself, but I've learned to trust my intuitive grasp of the social patterns I encounter. I can usually see what the overall pattern is, even if I can't defend my conclusions in a debate with a real expert.

"Forget this is supposed to represent people," I said. "Just think of it as forces and connections. This one over here is very powerful, but it has all these other forces tugging on it. These two are weaker, but they don't have a lot of forces acting on them, and they're both pulling in the same direction. What would you do if you wanted to get the red sphere in the center all the way to the right hand side of the screen?"

"Does the red one represent us?"

"It might."

She pointed at one of the larger spheres. "Weaken that one. Reduce its overall strength by about twenty percent."

"Have you got a second choice? Something that requires less of a change?"

"Does it have to be a certainty? You haven't told me the boundary conditions."

"Let's try for a high probability."

Her face tautened into the tight-stretched total concentration I had observed every time I had seen her coping with a crisis. Her hands moved across the screen as if she was physically trying out possibilities. We would have made an interesting visual study—she totally absorbed in what she was doing, me totally focused on her.

"That one," she said. "Can you make that one pull on the red sphere? If you can—then that one connects to this one… see? And this one is part of a group that.…"

She had ignored the two Xins I had been considering and pounced on another Xin named MyLien Thang. I hadn't thought of Talent Thang because her connections looked weak. Her strength lay in the way those weak connections plugged into networks that added up to something much more impressive. She was obviously an optimum choice—once someone like Ling traced the connections for you.

I spent two more hours arranging the contact and roughing in a draft of my approach message. Ling plugged her notescreen into a full-size desk screen and connected to one of her circles.

She turned her back on a screen full of mathematical symbols as soon as I told her dinner was ready, but you could tell she wasn't really interested in the array of bottles and edibles I had ordered up. "I think I'd better get my approach message polished up," I said after awhile. "I hope you don't mind if I concentrate on that for a couple of hours."

She looked confused. She had obviously been assuming she was going to spend the evening being polite to me. Then she recovered—it didn't take her long—and let me know there had been some interesting developments in one of her mathematical groups—stuff she was really going to have to work on if she wanted to grasp its implications. She even mouthed some words to the effect that she would really much rather spend the time with me.

It wasn't what I wanted, of course. I had activated one of my own modifications during the time we had spent on the bed. We had been joined together for nearly an hour, isolated in our own private universe. I would have kept it up for a dozen more hours if we had been embracing in a zero-g environment.

"I should advise you this really isn't my kind of thing," MyLien Thang said. "I almost slipped your letter into the polite refusal file as soon as I read it."

Talent Thang had conformed to the fashion by outfitting herself with a loose floor-length gown and hair that hung down her back to her waist. For her screen background she had chosen a subdued, gently colored floral arrangement.

"I've talked to some friends of mine who seemed to have the right connections," she said. "They managed to talk to a member of the Yan family, and he asked me to arbitrate this dispute. If that's acceptable to you, I'll bring their representative onscreen now."

"How does arbitration work? Is your decision final?"

"If you don't like my suggestions, you're both free to disregard them. I have no legal power in this. No member of the Conclave has. But our opinion usually carries some weight. I've only arbitrated three other disputes myself, but the Yan family said they wanted me to arbitrate, since I'm the Talent you contacted."

She paused for a moment, and I thought I picked up a little shimmer that flowed across her gown. It was only the slightest hint of a motion—the mere suggestion that a successful, fully elected politician had actually engaged in a *wiggle*.

"Please don't be optimistic, Mr. Baske. None of the people I talked to expressed much hope for you. I decided to go ahead because I'd spent an hour examining your history. You have a talent for adventuring and enjoying life. Our society can use some of that. I hope you'll consider staying on Mercury if we manage to get your present troubles straightened out. I can only help you, however, if I can work out something that has some general support."

I nodded. It was a variation on a theme I had heard before. Translation: one more woman had decided Joseph Louis Baske is a lovable scamp.

"I'll be happy to stay here for awhile if my companion and I can enjoy the freedoms your citizens normally enjoy."

She split the screen and presented us with a view of our friend Yan Daian. He was sitting in a wheelchair, naturally.

"Citizen Yan has already told me his views of the incident that brought this on," our arbitrator said. "Is there anything you'd like to add to the report you sent me? If you don't, I'm prepared to present my first suggestion."

I glanced at Ling. I wanted to take her hand, but it didn't seem like an appropriate gesture.

"I think I would like to hear your suggestion before I say anything else," I said.

"You are a stranger on our world," Talent Thang said. "While it's true that you physically attacked Yan Daian, it was your companion, Ling Chime, who instigated the actions that led to the attack. She was also the person who actually fired on two members of the Yan family and caused them extreme pain and bodily damage. Yan Daian has already indicated his family is willing to overlook your part in the affair, in return for a small token indemnity. Ling Chime's offense was much greater. From her, the Yan family demands an indemnity of three million yuris. In lieu of that, they will accept complete samples of all her tissues and body fluids, and a two-Eyear residency in their development facilities."

I stepped toward the screen. "That's absurd. The damage she did to the three members of the Yan family can be repaired in a few days. You're talking about a sum of money that represents years of her current salary."

"The Yan family do not permit people to attack them," Yan Daian said. "We cannot tolerate such behavior."

Ling was sitting in a lounge chair with her legs curled under her thighs and her notescreen perched on her lap. She lowered her head and started entering data with her stylus.

"Do you have anything to say to that, Ling Chime?" Talent Thang said.

"Give me two more minutes," Ling said. "If you don't mind."

Talent Thang stared at her. Ling had responded in exactly the same way she probably reacted when somebody interrupted her while she was pondering some aspect of her math interests.

"Yan Daian was deliberately obstructing traffic," I said. "Ling's employer was trying to make an important rendezvous before a fixed, unalterable deadline. How can—"

"I'll pay the indemnity," Ling said. "I've worked out a loan with the Third Traders Bank in Bangkok. Their Mercury alter has approved it."

I stepped up to her chair and studied her notescreen. The interest rate was nineteen point seven percent. "It will take you twenty-five Eyears to pay that back," I said. "Katrinka will have you under her thumb for over two decades."

"I'm not going to spend two Eyears in their laboratories."

"It seems like an exorbitant commitment to me, too," Talent Thang said. "Citizen Yan—if you reduced your demand to half a million yuris, Ling Chime would still have to spend over six Eyears paying off her debt. While she lived on a subsistence income."

"She should have thought of that before she subjected a member of my family to this indignity."

"You'll be restored to your normal condition in a tenday," I said. "And for that you think Ling should spend decades in a condition that amounts to penal servitude?"

"We are making you an offer, Mr. Baske. Talent Thang's friends asked us to make an offer, and we have. You don't have to accept it if you don't want to."

"It's settled, Joe," Ling said. "It's the best we can do."

"And what happens to us? Do I just let you leave here in a few days? Do I get on the ship with you and hope Katrinka will let me see you now and then after you get home?"

"You'll be preoccupied by someone else two tendays after I leave here. Even if I stayed, how long would it last? Two or three tendays?"

She was right, of course. The idyll I had in mind wouldn't last more than a few tendays. But nothing lasts. Every pleasure slips away from you. Does that mean you shouldn't value it?

I've met people who spent hefty fractions of their annual incomes traveling to places where they could spend a few hours listening to a certain opera. Should I deny my own hungers merely because I knew they would eventually be replaced by some other set of beauties and mysteries?

I picked up my notescreen and entered the code that generates an up-to-the-second summary from my financial alter. I already knew what the number was to within a few hundred yuris, but I never make a financial decision without getting a solid fix on that basic bit of information.

The alter would have to double my current wealth just to satisfy the Yan family's demands. I would have nothing left over for my own needs, even if it succeeded. Obviously I needed to try for something grander.

I turned back to Talent Thang. "Will you excuse me a few minutes? I'd like to investigate some possibilities."

"The situation has been resolved," Yan Daian said. "If Citizen Ling will just transfer her funds to our account, we'll all be able to resume our normal activities."

"I haven't agreed to the settlement. Is there any reason we have to rush through this, Talent Thang?"

"I'm certain we can spare a few minutes. I really think it would be best, Citizen Yan."

I backed out of the camera field and settled into the other lounge chair I had ordered for the suite. I had already entered the boundary conditions I was giving the alter. I wanted to end up with four and a half million: Ling's three million, plus the one and a half million I already had. A two hundred percent increase. Risk factor: seventy percent.

The alter came back with a zero response thirty seconds after I made the request. It always keeps an updated file of possible deals in memory. The time lag between Mercury and the big financial centers in the Earth-Moon system created problems, but Mercury had its own exchanges. Most of the currency derivatives I traded in the Earth-Luna exchanges could be traded on Mercury.

I stared at a pair of elegantly shaped vases that had been arranged beside the big wall screen. There was a moment when their slender lines seemed to be blurred by a mist. Then I pressed my stylus against the screen and entered a new risk factor: one hundred percent.

Ling hopped out of her chair. Her fingers grabbed my wrist before I could cover the notescreen with my hand.

"That's absurd," she said. "It's settled. I took a risk. I got us into trouble. You're just a bystander."

A list of deals appeared on the screen. I didn't understand any of them, of course. Those days were long gone. The only number that meant anything comprehensible was highlighted in red at the bottom of the screen. Probability of success: seventy-three percent.

She tightened her grip on my wrist as she turned her head toward the wall screen. "He's gambling his entire stock of capital. Isn't there some way you can lock up this arrangement so he'll stop?"

She didn't know it, but she was actually understating the situation. I had transformed most of my possessions into programs when I had left the Moon. My violin—one of my most treasured belongings—was just a bunch of numbers and instructions recorded in a molecular engineering file. So were my wines, three-fourths of my clothes, and most of the other items that make life tolerable. None of it could be reconstructed if I didn't have a single neil or yuri in my bank account.

"I've agreed to accept the proceeds of your loan," Yan Daian said. "If he wants to gamble so he can present you with a gift, that's his affair."

Ling's fingers pressed against the nerves of my left wrist. Her other hand snapped into action with all the speed her designers had coded into her nervous system. She backed away from the chair with my notescreen pressed against her hip.

"I'm not going to be responsible for your impoverishment. I'm not worth it."

I don't know what gave me the biggest surprise: the blurred movement or the blurted words.

"You certainly seemed worth it a few hours ago," I said. "I'm not exactly pining after an experience I haven't had yet."

"We've got days—whole Earthdays—before Katrinka leaves. We can have all of that we want."

"I don't want just that. I want to share your life. I want us to have the whole experience."

"There's no way you can share my life. Do you really think you can follow the kind of things I'm involved with? What difference would it make if you could? Do you have any idea what the people fifteen years younger than me are like? Do you understand what's happening with the children who are just being born?"

I frowned. I understood the first part of what she'd said. The second part sounded like irrelevant babbling. How could the brains and bodies coming out of the gene designers' shops have any effect on my relationship with the particular combination of genes and experience that had snared my emotions at this particular moment in my life?

I've met a number of men—hundreds by now, probably—who wanted to know the secret of my "success" with women. I usually tell them the big secret is the fact that I really am in love with every woman I pursue. But that's not the whole story. I've always had another talent—a gift for seeing the world through other people's eyes. The other people are usually female, of course. But that's a minor matter. The basic human emotions tend to be the same. Ling might be smarter than me. But I had been exploring the mysteries of the human personality for almost ninety years.

In some ways, I was looking at a creature from another world when I looked at young, super-enhanced people like Ling. But that didn't change the emotions that any organism will feel when it's faced with certain circumstances. When you're threatened, you become frightened. When you can't do anything about a threat—when you can't fight or run—you become depressed.

I had thought her coolness under fire was an aspect of her general competence. But now I understood it could also be a sign her emotions had been flattened by the terrible knowledge that she had become obsolete on the day she was born.

I didn't understand all of this immediately, of course. I worked some of it out later. But I could see the outlines of it. And I could form another hypothesis. When people grab a subject out of nowhere and throw it into an emotional argument, it's usually a sign they're trying to tell you something. It may even be an indication they're *asking* you for something.

"Is that what's bothering you?" I said. "Is that the real reason you're wasting your abilities working for someone like Katrinka? Is that why you're playing around with ideas? Instead of making them the central focus of your life?"

"Doesn't it bother you? Haven't you grasped what's happening?"

"In thirty years—fifty years—sometime in the foreseeable future—I'm going to be sharing the Solar System with people who have brains that will probably make me look like an imbecile by comparison. And so will you. So will the people being born today probably."

"You aren't going to *share* it with them. You're going to be *replaced* by them."

I pushed myself out of the chair and stepped in front of the main screen. "Talent Thang—will you please link me with my notescreen?"

"Of course."

She put a replica of my notescreen on the bottom half of her screen, and I immediately gave it my current password. The alter program intoned the traditional reminder that past performance is no guarantee of future success —one of the more tiresome mantras the lawyer class has inflicted on human society—and I gave it an execution order. Then I turned back to Ling.

"No one is going to *replace* me," I said. "Not in any sense that means anything important. They can't *feel* for me. They can't *live my life* for me. They can't change the way I felt when I held your shoulders in my hands and saw your eyes looking up at me."

"Are you trying to make me grateful? Is that it? You're hoping I'll stay on Mercury after Katrinka leaves just because I feel grateful?"

"I'm hoping you'll stay here because you want to. And because you have the opportunity."

"You're risking everything you own just so you can have a temporary frolic with someone you hardly know."

"I'm hoping I'll have a kind of experience I've had before—the kind of experience I can have when someone makes me feel the way you make me feel."

"How long is this going to take?" Yan Daian said. "It seems to me we've settled everything we were supposed to settle."

"I suggest you stay with us, Citizen Yan," Talent Thang said. "If Mr. Baske doesn't object, I can even put my image of his program on your screen and let you monitor his progress."

"This is a private matter between him and her. We've already arrived at a settlement."

"It would still be best if you stayed. I'm certain your family would agree with me."

It only took the alter ten minutes to get my total wealth above four million. But a minute later the total dropped back to three-sixty. From there it started bouncing between three million two hundred thousand and three million nine hundred thousand.

No one talked much. Even Yan Daian started showing signs he was becoming absorbed in the numbers. Ling had dropped into a chair. Her hands were gripped between her knees. Her eyes had turned into slits—as if she was trying to limit her sensory input to the bare minimum.

The bottom line crossed the four million mark for the second time just twenty minutes after I'd actuated the program. Then it started down again.

"I think you'd better stop, Mr. Baske," Talent Thang said. "Please consider that an official request—based on my judgment of what seems to be happening."

I studied her face for a moment and decided this would be a good time to yield to higher authority. I gave the alter the word, and it closed out its positions at three million, eight hundred thousand.

"Are we done?" Yan Daian asked.

"Mr. Baske is seven hundred thousand yuris short of the amount he needs to pay Citizen Ling's debt. He has engaged in one of the most extraordinary acts I've ever witnessed. As a member of the Conclave of Talents—as somebody responsible for maintaining the peace and general civility of our society—I believe you would be doing everyone a service if you reduced Citizen Ling's indemnity by that amount."

Yan Daian raised one of his long arms above his head and studied his palm. "It's not my fault he needs a better alter."

"This incident has already come to the attention of a number of people who are connected to your family. You are not without fault yourself, Citizen Yan. I have reason to believe your family would probably feel you had done the right thing if you exercised some leniency at this moment. I haven't met your mother personally. But I have several friends who have. From what they've told me, she would be a much happier woman if they could advise her you exercised some good judgment at this moment...."

My time with Ling didn't end after three or four tendays, as we had both assumed. It lasted over three Mercury years—almost all of an Earth year. It concluded with a touch of comedy that amused both of us.

I left Ling alone with her screens one day and a musical, slightly ironic laugh attracted my attention. I spent most of a tenday wondering how I could tell Ling about the relationship I was developing with the woman who owned the musical laugh. And discovered—as I should have expected—that Ling had been putting off the sad day when she would have to tell me she had established a community with three people in her cosmology circle. They had all agreed, it seemed, that they should set up an in-person household on a "promising-looking research habitat the Kwan-Bain Cooperative is placing in a long-duration cometary orbit." Ling had already purchased her passage to the habitat, in fact. She had meant to tell me before she made her reservations, but…

It hadn't been quite the idyll I had envisioned. Ling spent at least half of every day in front of her screens. She had left the rest of it up to me, however. I gave her dinners she would never have arranged for herself. I showed her how we could both take full advantage of the possibilities created by her dimmed sexual responses. I put some of my capital into a small partnership and showed her she could live quite comfortably without indenturing herself to someone like Katrinka Yamioto Oldaf-Li. Ling had never really looked at the financial markets. She had just assumed they were too risky.

And, of course, we talked. All real love affairs involve three things: sexual union, shared experience, and talk.

Ling had been eleven when she had begun to understand her true situation. Up until then, she had thought of herself as someone who had been given special gifts, thanks to her parents. "Then I went through this period where I got really fascinated by Go. I spent two hundred hours working with mentor programs. I ate meals in front of my screens so I could play in tournaments. Then one day I ran into somebody who left me feeling totally confused. The only thing I really understood about the game was the fact that I'd lost. And I discovered I'd been playing someone who was only six."

She only talked about the subject when we were lying in bed, with our bodies arranged so she didn't have to look at me while she talked. This was the first time she'd talked about it with someone who wasn't a member of her own age group. "The essence of intelligence is the ability to predict the future. I couldn't tell my parents how I felt. They'd practically beggared themselves so I could have the best. But all the people my own age could figure it out. The numbers indicated intelligence was going up about twenty percent every nine years. It was going to double about every thirty years."

"So you just created a little hideaway for yourself. And stepped out of the mainstream of life."

"I didn't know what to do. None of us do. I couldn't see it the way you do. I'd spent my childhood thinking I was the next step in human evolution. And suddenly it turns out I'm just a tiny little interim phase."

It was one of those relationships in which two people exchange bits of their personalities. Ling was glowing with anticipation when she transmitted her last message from her couch on the ground-to-orbit shuttle. I think I can say she had discovered she could enjoy life and pursue her own pleasures even if she knew someone "better" was going to inhabit the Solar System in the not-too-distant future. She had shaken off her torpor and recognized there are aspects of life that are just as important as intelligence and competence.

As for me—I had finally been forced to concede that the gulf she was worried about was very real. There was going to come a day when the Solar System would be full of intelligent, physically magnificent women who would think of me as a rather crude prototype. I had always made contact with the minds and personalities of the women I loved. Someday that would be impossible.

The woman with the unforgettable laugh was a survivor from the middle of the 20th Century—the only member of that rare company I have ever become involved with. She had outlasted two bouts with cancer in the days when tumors were assaulted with powerful chemical poisons. Sometime in her eighties, thirty years after the new century had begun, she had discovered she wasn't living in the last years of her life after all. She had dodged all the traps that could have killed her and reached a time when she could start her life all over again.

She had heard about me, of course. I think she took me up mostly out of curiosity. She looked at the world around her with the arch, slightly detached viewpoint of a tourist from a remote, immeasurably alien country. Her laugh was even more ironic—and just as musical—when she moved in my arms as she responded to the elation flooding her senses.

When she had been a student, near the middle of the 20th Century, she had studied the literature of England and the United States. It was the subject conventional young women studied in the United States in those days. She liked to quote a 17th Century poet named Andrew Marvell. *Had we but world enough and time, this coyness, Lady, were no crime.*

We had lived into an era when we had several worlds, she pointed out. And much time. And coyness was no longer fashionable.

ROMANCE WITH PHOBIC VARIATIONS

She taught me much and gave me very
sound advice; which if I had only followed
it my life would not have been stormy, and
so I should not today have found it worth recording.
—Giacomo Casanova, *History of My Life*, tr. Willard R. Trask

The two desperados on the screen had obviously made a serious investment in modifications that maximized their muscle mass. No naturally occurring gene had ever generated the kind of deltoids and biceps they were displaying. The fashions on Phobos tended to be lush and dressy, but they had opted for a style that reminded me of the careless, deliberately slovenly clothing people had affected when I had been a boy at the turn of the millennium. The main item in their ensemble was a loose, short-sleeved pullover that hung straight down from their shoulders to just above their knees. Their heads were crowned with skullcaps that contained obscenities written in most of the languages commonly used in the off-Earth communities.

"We have a message for your friend," one of them said. "From the associates who were kind enough to lend her some working capital."

I straightened up. It had been approximately four hours since I had told Aki Nento I would call her creditors and see if I could bluff them into leaving her alone. She had begged me not to do it. Money was the only thing that could influence them, she had said. If I really wanted to help her, I should lend her more money.

Now I was face to face with a couple of rockbodies who apparently represented the very people I had hoped to threaten. Only they were doing the threatening.

"If you're speaking of the person I think you're referring to," I said, "she's already received a number of messages from her creditors."

"We think she might pay more attention if you relayed the message. You might even be doing yourself a favor. The people we represent are afraid you might be a bad influence on her. They'd have a better opinion of you if you offered them a contrary indicator."

"Nento is engaged in a speculative business venture. Her creditors knew they were investing in something risky. Their behavior is absurd."

"They loaned her money. People who borrow money should pay it back."

"They loaned her money so she could invest it in a speculative project. They knew what the project was. They knew it might not work out exactly as planned. It was a legitimate business transaction. It should be dealt with as a legitimate business transaction."

The hoodlum on the left had been glowering while the hoodlum on the right talked. The hoodlum on the left opened his mouth and the hoodlum on the right switched to glowering mode.

"The kind of people we're talking about always get something back. They get their money back. Or they get something else. That's all you have to tell her."

They terminated the call, and I settled into a chair as soon as I realized I was staring at a blank screen. It wasn't the first time I had been threatened by the products of modern biological craftsmanship. The first one I had encountered had been a woman—a female killing machine with a body and a personality that had been shaped by designers who had started with the DNA in an unfertilized egg. These two looked like they had just given themselves a superficial remodeling. I would still be as helpless as a caterpillar if they ever got me cornered.

The situation didn't make any sense. Nento had borrowed the money so she could design chase robots that could function on Mars. In spite of all the evidence to the contrary, she had assumed the Martian population included thousands of people who would like to whoop across the Martian landscape in pursuit of simulated versions of boars, dragons, and other real and mythological creatures. I didn't think it was such a great idea myself, but people who loaned out capital were supposed to have some business sense. They didn't start threatening you with bodily harm when a scheme didn't start producing profits at the exact moment specified in the contract.

I had said that to Nento when she had asked me for a second loan. I had already helped her meet a payment date. My financial alter would start nagging me with warning messages if I yielded to Nento's pleas and made another dent in my capital.

"This is ridiculous," I had said. "I'll talk to them. I've got a few connections myself. I'll let them know they could be in serious trouble if they carried out any of their threats."

Nento's bright little eyes widened. "I can't let you do that, Joe. You don't know who you're dealing with. The people I borrowed from—they aren't the kind of people I usually do business with."

I had been threatened before, but that didn't mean I could smile cheerfully and ignore all the pain and damage the two paragons of muscle worship could inflict on me. I had still been planning my approach to Nento's creditors when I had accepted their call. I had been visualizing the expressions that would cross their faces when they discovered they were inconveniencing a woman who had captured the fancy of the renowned

Joseph Louis Baske. Now *I* was the one who was sitting in his parlor struggling with an unexpected attack of anxiety and dismay.

The Voice of the apartment broke into my emotional fog. A visitor was standing at my door.

The screen lit up, and I found myself looking at another triumph of modern biology. This one was almost as tall as the two toughs, and several times brighter. He was also better dressed. If he had straightened up his shoulders and acted like he had a normal supply of self-confidence, his white jacket and his embroidered sash would have made him look like a young prince. Unfortunately, he was only fifteen years old. He was slouching inside his clothes as if the microgravity of Phobos had drained all the energy out of his muscles.

I eyed him with a mixture of pleasure and embarrassment. His name was Sori Dali, and he was the son of a gracious, wonderfully civilized woman named Denava Dali. Two tendays ago, his mother and I had been planning a liaison that should have lasted most of a Martian year.

"I have to see you," Sori said. "I've got something important to show you, Joe."

I stood up and greeted him as he came through the door. I had increased my height by sixteen percent just before I had left Mercury, but he was still over two heads taller. I had been a little taller than average height when I had reached my full growth back in the Teens. Then I had slowly lost ground as the century wore on. Now, after eighty years, I was back where I had started.

He had brought a file card with him. He inserted it into my screen, and faces started flashing past us.

"These are the faces of forty-one of the women you've been in love with in the last thirty-two years. I collected every picture I could locate in the databanks."

Memories prodded my emotions. Every face in the parade evoked a response—pleasure, pain, excitement, tenderness, melancholy. Some of them had reigned over interludes that only lasted one or two days. One had captivated me for forty-five minutes. Others had shared a companionship and intimacy that lasted for months and years. It didn't matter. They were all part of an adventure that has bathed my life in color and warmth.

"Now watch," Sori said.

A new set of faces flitted across the screen. They all looked vaguely familiar, but none of them seemed to be associated with a name or a memory. Some of them were so haunting they actually aroused a feeling of longing as they vanished after their moment on the screen.

The last item in the series jolted me as if I'd been clubbed. Nento stared at me with her eyes glittering with life. The program turned her head to one side, and she raised her chin and regarded me with a smiling, sidewise look that had been befuddling me for most of the last two tendays.

"I set up a program that made random composites based on the characteristics of the real women. Every time I've run it, it eventually produced this one."

The picture wasn't an exact replica of Nento. When you looked at it for a few seconds, you could see the differences. Nento's face was a little rounder. Her nose was a shade longer, her lips a little fuller.

"I know it's not a perfect resemblance," Sori said. "They probably used more pictures than I did. I suppose, too, there are limits on the changes you can inflict on a real person. Now look at this—this is what Nento looked like one Eyear ago."

He was talking very fast, with little gasps for breath. I could smell the way he was sweating. He knew what he was doing to me.

The original Nento had a noticeably fuller face. Her lips formed a fleshy pout—a feature that seems to appeal to men who are looking for childlike, compliant sex partners. The face I knew had captivated me with lines that suggested a refined, controlled forcefulness. The face on the screen would have attracted a casual glance at most.

"If you look up the data associated with this face in the public databanks, you'll discover they've made some changes in her biography, too. I think we can also be confident they instituted some extensive temporary personality modifications. All the information in the databanks indicates you feel a woman's personality is just as important as her appearance. You react to faces, in fact, because you feel certain facial characteristics are associated with certain personality characteristics."

"I looked up Nento's personal biography," I said. "I always do."

"Did you look for news stories? You probably searched for her name, right? I worked backward from the face the composite program gave me.

I did a visual search, looking for facial characteristics that matched the face they probably started with."

He pulled his card out of my screen and gave me some relief from the sight of Nento's true identity. "Somebody set a trap for you, Joe. They probably read the passenger lists. They probably knew you were coming here from Mercury. They designed a woman you couldn't resist. I wouldn't be surprised to learn they created a model of your personality structure, too. The information on you in the public databanks would support a model that would be adequate for their purposes."

I have devoted my life to the peculiar combination of emotional and sensual pleasure we humans call love. I believe I can honestly say I have been in love with every woman I have ever pursued. The things I do with the women I love are no different from the things most people do. In spite of all the fantasies created by pornographers, there really aren't that many possibilities. The things I feel, however, make every adventure an experience to treasure. The emotion is temporary. It never lasts. But it is a real emotion, nonetheless. I have followed my heart wherever it led me.

Now Sori was telling me someone had taken the central passion of my life and turned it against me. It was the most disorienting moment I have ever experienced. One part of my personality was outraged. The rest of it was still responding to all the complex emotions Nento aroused.

Usually, I can describe the response a woman is evoking, in the same way I can describe my response to a piece of music. With Sori's mother, the dominant appeal had been graciousness and serenity—a combination that had seemed like the perfect antidote to the turbulence of my last adventures on Mercury. The Mercurian habitat was a huge, world-circling structure, with over half a billion inhabitants, but it had developed a social network that was so intricate I couldn't become involved with a woman without tripping over all the relationships created by my previous affairs.

I had encountered Denava Dali and her son two days after I had arrived on Phobos. I had been captivated when I heard them talking while they stood by one of the public viewscreens and observed the passage of the Martian landscape, ten thousand kilometers below us. Then—when Denava and I had been sitting in a cafe planning our next pleasure—I had looked at the table next to us and seen Nento. And found myself yielding to an emotional assault that was so complicated it made me feel like I was reacting to a Bach fugue.

It had been an embarrassing moment. Normally, a new woman doesn't attract me until the charms of the old one begin to fade. This was the first time I had been pulled away from a banquet that was just beginning.

Every time I looked at Nento—every time I *thought* about her—a dozen different emotions seemed to be interacting at the same time. The tilt of her chin held out a promise of challenge and revelry. The precise, graceful movements of her hands and the trim, subtly softened curve of her waist and hips added grace notes of elan and undertones of warmth and sensuality. When we had settled into our first real conversation, I had quickly discovered she was an irresistible mixture of the mature pleasure-loving coquette and the able woman of achievement. Every facet of her appearance and her personality seemed to be sending me a different message.

Could it really be true? Could they really predict the kind of woman who would exercise that kind of power over me? Could they really shape someone so she would fulfill all the requirements of the prediction?

But of course they could. The human race had been dealing with the ramifications of personality modification technology for over four decades. Twenty years earlier, when I had been tormented by a woman who had no interest in anything I had to offer, I had even considered using it on myself.

"Your lifestyle makes you particularly vulnerable," Sori said. "You are committed to following your romantic impulses. You may want to consider a different approach in this case."

I stared at him through a haze of conflicting emotions. "She doesn't exist," I said. "She never did exist."

"Did she get any money out of you?"

"What difference does that make? Do you know what you're telling me?"

"But you have given her money?"

"I gave her a loan to help her deal with her creditors. Do you have any idea what this means to me? Is there any difference between telling me this and telling me she's dead?"

"I did some investigating after I found her face. She's a professional swindler—part of a three-woman trio. It looks like they've been working the tourists for the last couple of Eyears. I think I could help you get your money back. You might even get a little of theirs. I've been working on personality models ever since I was a child. I've already done some preliminary work on a model of her. We might work out an approach that would help us reverse the situation, if you'd help me get some more information on her."

His mother had paid for a genetic workup that had given him the best brain and the best general physiology the market could provide. If he had been playing around with personality models for the last six or seven years, he probably had the equivalent of a full professional degree in the subject.

I had only known him for four tendays, but we had hit it off from the start. His hyped-up physiology included a full set of male glands. He was right at the age when his hormones were racing through his arteries in full flood, and he was enduring all that sweet, lovely turmoil in a time when girls his own age were almost as rare as people who suffered from genetic disabilities. His mother had been fifty-six when she had finally decided she wanted to explore the satisfactions of parenthood. She had done it right. She had every right to be pleased with herself. But she had produced an adolescent son who was surrounded by desirable women—and male rivals—who were, at minimum, two or three decades older than he was.

I had been giving him the best advice I could. For all his intelligence, he had been misled by the foolishness that besets many young men. He had assumed a woman was a prize who could be won by demonstrating your virtues. In his case, that was a recipe for failure. None of the women he met on Phobos were going to be dazzled by his worldly sophistication or his ability to pontificate on important intellectual matters. I was slowly convincing him he had to work with his weaknesses. He should give them the pleasure of leading an inexperienced young man through his first sexual adventures.

I bent at the knees and pushed myself toward the ceiling with my arms over my head. On Earth, when I was young, we used to say an agitated person was bouncing off the walls. On worlds like Phobos, you can actually do it.

Sori had found records that indicated Nento and her two accomplices had been working a gambling scheme. They pretended they were strangers and drew a victim into a four-way backgammon game. The dupe thought he and his partner were playing against another twosome. He didn't realize he was playing against three other people and they would split the proceeds when they had emptied his bank account. The victim was always a he, of course. The fact that the other three players were easygoing, well-endowed women tended to numb his critical faculties. If he made too much noise after he realized what had happened, they spent a small percentage of their profits, and employed the services of the two enforcers who had just called me.

"I think we can take it for granted there are no creditors threatening Nento," Sori said. "Your callers were undoubtedly engaging in a charade for the benefit of Nento and her partners."

Sori had been five years old when he had realized the people around him were not operating at random, even if they weren't totally rational. His mother had referred to the science of psychology when she had been trying to explain someone's behavior, and he had looked up the subject in his encyclopedia. One Eyear later, he had entered a few observations into his notescreen and constructed a model that correctly predicted her newest male acquaintance liked to eat melons for breakfast.

"The motivations of people who engage in criminal and antisocial behavior have been rather thoroughly mapped," Sori said. "It was one of the first subjects personality modelers placed on their agenda. There are only approximately six reasons why people are attracted to swindling crimes. If you'll just visit Nento two more times—perhaps three—and record her responses to certain actions, I should be able to eliminate the motivations that aren't applicable, and construct an accurate picture of the emotions we should work with."

It was a dangerous idea. Could I really sit in the same room with Nento and coolly execute Sori's instructions? If Sori was right about her, I should hop on the next spaceship to the asteroid belt and put two hundred million kilometers between us as soon as possible.

So why did I let myself accede to Sori's schemes? At that moment, buffeted by an emotional whirlwind, I think I did it primarily because I would still have a relationship with Nento if I participated in his maneuverings. It might be a perverse relationship, but it was better than no relationship at all.

It was the first time a woman had made me feel that way. I'd met a few teasers who kept pretending they might eventually yield to my stratagems, just so they could keep me pursuing them. None of them inspired thoughts of revenge, no matter how angry they made me. They had toyed with my feelings because they had taken an emotional pleasure out of being courted. They hadn't turned themselves into traps so they could add a few more neils and yuris to their bank accounts.

Nento was all smiles when she came on the screen. Her eyes deepened with sympathy when I described my conversation with the two intimidators. If I hadn't seen Sori's evidence, I would never have suspected my oversized callers had been carrying out instructions they had received from her and her accomplices.

"You did your best, Joe. I'm certain you did your best. Phobos is one of the most lawless places I've encountered. It looks civilized, but people like that can do almost anything they want."

I couldn't argue with her about that. Phobos had a government of sorts, complete with courts and a police force, but it was controlled by three political factions, and the members of all three were mostly interested in the bribes and fees they could collect. I had browsed through the information Sori had collected. If Phobos had been run by a real government, Nento and her two colleagues would have been paying serious penalties.

Sori had scripted the exact words I should use when I told her I wanted to see her again. I repeated them as instructed, and we cycled into the pattern that had been driving me insane for twenty days. Her work was becoming terribly demanding, Nento maintained. Perhaps she could give me twenty minutes just before her dinner appointment. She couldn't see me for lunch tomorrow, but she had an hour right after lunch the day after that....

Usually I pursue a woman by placing myself in the right position and letting one thing lead to another. With Nento, I had told her how I felt the first time I was alone with her.

"That's very flattering," she had said. "Are you telling me I have become the current obsession of the famous Joseph Louis Baske—a man who has been compared to the legendary Giacomo Casanova?"

She had been looking at me out of the corner of her eye, with her head tipped back and a smile playing around her face—a look I was going to see a hundred times in the future. I knew she was going to be a problem. I knew she was pulling me back into the turbulence that had ended my sojourn on Mercury. It didn't matter. Nento had implanted an ache that nagged me like a chronic illness. I wanted her. I wanted to touch her. I wanted to hold her. I wanted to look at her.

I shared a couch with her during the twenty minutes she had granted me before her "dinner appointment," and the ache grew stronger all the time I was there. The hour two days later was just as difficult. I managed to recite the scripts Sori had given me, but it all seemed irrelevant. Why should I care how she reacted when I knocked over a glass of wine? What difference did it make if she laughed and said "red and yellow" when I asked her what kind of flowers she liked?

I held her for a long minute at the end of our twenty-minute rendezvous. She chuckled with pleasure when she nuzzled me during the session that lasted one entire heady hour. In my current state, that was all that mattered.

Her responses evoked satisfied nods from Sori. He sent me back one more time, to settle some doubts he had, and made his pronouncement.

"She's primarily interested in dominating people. She probably sees herself as a kind of hidden center of power, operating the controls that make other people do what she wants."

I had acquired some skill with sociological models. They can be very useful when your chosen lifestyle bounces you from one social milieu to another. Personality models were another matter. I understood the rudiments, but most of the vectors and symbols on Sori's screens were meaningless lines and blobs.

But what did you do with the model after you had it? Sori could map Nento's motivations, but I was the one who created a scheme that would exploit them.

"I gather you find Nento attractive," I said.

He put on his best man-of-the-world air. "I wouldn't turn her down if she made me an offer."

"It seems to me we should let you be the target. We can tell her you've come up with a new scheme for playing the currency markets—something that could only be devised by someone with your intellectual powers. Normally, you only work with clients who have very large sums of money. Since you find her desirable, however…"

"And then I let her feel she's getting me under control. She invests some money with me, and we let her get a profit, right? Then we let her raise the investment. And my marvelous, secret wonder-method suddenly fails."

I smiled politely. His eyes had widened and he was talking with the overheated rush he fell into whenever an interesting new idea popped into his brain. I had planned a detailed briefing, complete with little lectures on the fundamentals of the swindler's art. Somehow, I always seemed to underestimate his abilities.

Nento maintained an air of studied coolness when I told her I had stumbled onto a way she could raise money herself. She frowned—a very fetching frown—when I suggested Sori might grant her access to his investment programs because she appealed to his youthful longings.

"Are you suggesting I should use sexual attraction to help me acquire *money*, Joe? That doesn't sound like you."

"He's a young boy," I said. "He's only fifteen. I'm merely suggesting he might be willing to make an exception in your case and give you a temporary spot on his client list. He'd probably think you were doing him a big favor if you just talked to him on the phone for ten minutes."

"I'm still surprised you'd even suggest such a thing. I didn't think women who behaved that way appealed to you."

I bypassed her protests by launching into a description of Sori's financial success, complete with reports that indicated he had been making ten to thirty percent every five tendays, with no periods in which he had suffered a loss. The reports were modified versions of the achievements of my own financial alter. They looked authentic, and for the most part they were. My alter is about as good as they get. I buy every upgrade that looks worthwhile as soon as I feel it has proved itself. I had merely eliminated most of the down days when I had made up the reports.

"It certainly does sound intriguing," Nento said. "Do you think he might be interested if I approached him with a straight business proposition? I could offer him a share in my business, for example, in exchange for a place on his client list."

She really was an accomplished actress. At that point in its history, Mars was mostly inhabited by researchers, conservationists, and a small number of people who were studying various terraforming schemes. None of them, it seemed to me, sounded like people who wanted to go tallyhoing after robots. Phobos had become a major tourist point because they had lobbied for laws that discouraged travelers who wanted to visit Mars for frivolous purposes. She couldn't possibly believe a financial genius would take a serious interest in her business proposal.

Sori was almost as disoriented as I was when he finished her first call. She kept him on the screen for almost two hours. She started out with a pure business approach and slowly switched to something more effective. She gave him the same out-of-the-corner-of-the-eyes looks she gave me. She got up from behind her desk and let him admire the long, elegant lines of her hips and thighs as she walked around. She smiled at the way he reacted to her and let him know she didn't mind it at all.

Naturally, she made him promise he wouldn't discuss their relationship with me.

"Joe is a very nice man," Nento said. "He's a little over-experienced, if you know what I mean. But I think his feelings should be treated with care."

"I'll do whatever you want," Sori affirmed. "Just tell me what you want."

He stopped the recording at that point when he played it for me. "Watch the flash in her eyes," he said when he played it back. "See. Right there."

"I saw it. You don't have to know much about human nature to guess what she's feeling."

"In the past, criminal behavior was always associated with motives like dominance or self-esteem, in addition to pure economic motives. The balance between economic motives and psychological motives has apparently shifted in the last few decades, as the spread of fabricators and molecular technology has affected human attitudes. Now that we can all live very pleasant lives without spending money, the psychological motives have apparently become dominant and the economic motives have become secondary."

I once spent an arduous period tramping through Peru with an ethnologist. Sori reacted to the things he learned about people in the same way she had reacted to the things she learned about the mating behavior of tree frogs. Discoveries that would be obvious to anyone over thirty-five were big revelations to Denava's genetically enhanced offspring.

And underneath it all, he was still basically an adolescent male plagued by the most powerful hungers evolution has bestowed on our species. Nento could have maneuvered him as if he was a robot. Fortunately, I was the one who handled the money. We combined Nento's test money with my capital, and my alter maintained its winning streak. I topped off her real profit with an extra ten percent, just to make it look juicier, and her eyes gleamed again.

Sori didn't give in too easily, of course. He had held out for a day or so before he let her make a test investment, and he wavered again when she told him she wanted to put in a bigger sum. His system didn't work well with small amounts, he claimed. He was risking a big loss when he added such a trivial quantity to his capital.

I'm not a jealous person. All my loves eventually end. Why should I become insanely angry if the object of my desires enjoys some variety, too? Why should I care if a manipulative little thief exploits her charms for another dupe? In Nento's case, none of my normal reactions seemed to be functioning. Nento responded to his delays with a long session in her apartment, and I spent three hours bouncing around my apartment and thinking about the soothing concoctions I could create with the fabricator I had purchased when I landed on Phobos. I had left my old personal fabricator on Mercury, to save weight charges. The programs packaged with the new one included a huge menu of psychoactive drinks.

Sori looked quite pleased with the world when he gave me his report. "I have to say, Joe, I'm beginning to understand your lifestyle. There are worse ways to spend your life, aren't there?"

"I take it you enjoyed yourself, then?"

"Oh, yes."

"And how did our business arrangements go?"

He smiled. "I let her know I would reconsider my objections to her investment hopes and give her my answer the next time we met. She informed me that wasn't at all satisfactory, and indicated she might not be free to see me again if I didn't submit to her financial demands. And I reluctantly accepted her transfer of the sum you and I had hoped to wrest from her."

"So we have her."

"*We* have her economically. *I*, my good friend…"

"I understand. Enjoy your memories."

"If it hadn't been for you, Joe…"

"I understand, Sori."

I cut him off and conjured up the liquid that offered me the fastest form of chemical escape.

The sums we were dealing with would have looked absurdly small when I was young. The molecular technology revolution had made me glad I earned my living investing in currencies instead of equities.

The fabricator had obviously made some uses of money almost obsolete. Who needed money when you could create food, clothing, and most of the necessities of life merely by inserting common substances into a fabricator equipped with the proper programs? On the other hand—what did you do to earn money when so many things could be acquired without labor? A table in a good restaurant still cost money—even if I could create the same food myself. So did fashion. My tastes in clothes are reasonably sober, but I'm not going to run around in garments created with out-of-date bootleg programs.

So Nento and I each had something in common. The money was important, but it wasn't the main reason we were trying to bilk each other. I had spent a bigger percentage of my working capital on other women and received just as little in return. For me, the true reward was the moment when I put Nento on my phone screen and told her Sori's program had returned one of its failures.

Her response was a look of pure horror. "You told me he was a financial genius. You said his system never failed."

"Every system fails now and then. Nobody can invent a system that can predict the fluctuations in the markets with perfect accuracy."

"I have to get that money back, Joe. You have to lend me more money. *You don't know what you've done to me.*"

"The amount you invested is a very small percentage of the sums you claim you owe your creditors, Nento. It can't possibly make that big a difference."

"You don't understand! That money belonged to some friends of mine. *I was supposed to be holding it for them.*"

I had assumed she was acting. Now I was beginning to think she really was terrified. I had never seen the two female accomplices Sori had mentioned, but I had assumed they had been lurking in the background while Nento attempted to manipulate me. Had she taken money she was supposed to share with them and invested it in Sori's mythical system? Had she tried to make a little profit on the side without mentioning it to them? I could see how she could be in serious trouble if she had.

"You have to help me, Joe! Don't desert me. Don't leave me alone."

I had been imagining an immensely satisfying scene: she would be the bewildered dupe and I would be the master schemer who had outwitted her. Instead, I was looking at a woman who seemed to be in serious trouble. Suppose I gave her—as a gift—the money I had just wiggled away from her? It was the same sum she had originally taken from me, but this time I might actually get something back in return.

Was she capable of gratitude? Would she just take the money and resume her campaign to get everything else I had?

"You'll have to tell me the details, Nento. How much trouble are you really in? If—"

Sori stepped up to the screen and switched it off. "That's it, Joe. She'll have you begging her to take everything you own if you keep on talking to her."

"She's in real trouble. That's not an act."

"It's not your responsibility. She's a thief and a prostitute. She's spent her life creating the same kind of trouble for other people."

"That's not the way you sounded the other day."

"I'm not like you, Joe. Your sexual feelings are associated with a strong measure of the emotions humans are referring to when they say they're in love—tenderness, idealization, affection, companionship, concern for the other person's welfare. According to most theorists, those emotions evolved because primitive humans had to create bonds that would keep them together during the long period required to raise a human infant to full social maturity. In your case, the so-called romantic emotions don't seem to last long enough to create the desired effect. But they seem to be exceptionally strong while they last."

"And you don't feel that tendency to create bonds?"

"Not in Nento's case. I enjoyed the interlude I spent with her. I would certainly like to repeat it. But I have no interest in her outside of the sexual pleasure I enjoyed with her."

He left me, and I once again found myself coping with a cauldron of emotions. This time I turned to an escape that had been one of my chief consolations for over sixty years. I had installed my first musical performance system in my nervous system back in the '30s, during one of my happiest affairs. The system had given me so much pleasure I had installed one or two upgrades every decade since then. Just before I left Mercury, I had purchased a fabricator program that reproduced one of the finest violins made in the 17th Century—a Nicolas Amati with a lively response and a tone that captured the noblest qualities of Baroque musical culture. I turned my attention to Bach's great ciaconne in D minor and spent the next forty minutes totally immersed in the challenges and mysteries of its thirty-one variations.

It was a wonderful vacation, but my internal chaos took possession of me minutes after I put down my bow. Could I really regard any woman with the detached objectivity Sori had displayed when he had described his attitude toward Nento? Nento was an artificial construct, but she was still a human being. The emotions she aroused were real emotions.

The Voice of the apartment interrupted my brooding. The two gentlemen with muscular physiques had an urgent message for me.

They had discarded the slovenly look. This time they were dressed in the height of fashionable dandyism, complete with high-collared tunics that held their necks militarily erect. The one on the right initiated their spiel.

"We don't know how well you understand the situation here on Phobos, Honored Baske. We should advise you that certain kinds of behavior are generally handled privately, between the parties involved, without the time-consuming procedures required by the court system. In most cases involving the kind of behavior you've engaged in, the court system will support the results of the private settlement."

"I'm afraid I have no idea what you're talking about," I said. "Exactly what type of behavior are you referring to?"

"You and your accomplice, Sori Dali, conspired to relieve Aki Nento of the sum of twenty thousand neils by fraudulently claiming you were investing her money in the currency markets. You retained the money instead and fraudulently advised her you lost it."

"We have no reason to doubt the accuracy of the claim," the fop on the left said. "Nento has shown us a recording of a conversation between her and your alleged accomplice. He described the whole scheme to her in some detail."

"Sori is only fifteen years old. He would say almost anything to an appealing woman at this stage in his life."

"We would advise you to stay in your apartment until you are prepared to return the sum you stole from your victim, with a ten percent addition to cover our participation in this matter. We have full legal access to the public surveillance system."

I called Sori as soon as they cut off, and his screen told me it would be glad to take a message. I called again ten minutes later and got his mother. We exchanged stiff, awkward greetings, and she called Sori to the phone.

"I just got a call from the two hoodlums who tried to threaten me earlier. Did you really tell Nento what we'd done?"

"They called me right after they called you," Sori said. "I was worried about you, Joe. I could tell you couldn't stand up to her if she kept after you. I called her up so I could tell her we knew all about her. I thought she might leave you alone if she realized we know what she is."

"And while you were at it, you told her how we'd duped her."

"I thought it might convince her she couldn't outmaneuver us."

"Did your model of her tell you that's how she'd react?"

"I didn't use the model. It isn't that complete."

"And now I can't leave my apartment without an all-out assault by a pair of giants. And neither can you, I presume. Or your mother. They have full legal access to every surveillance camera in every corridor and public space on this entire moon."

"I understand that, Joe. I'm working on a solution."

"What are you going to do—find some way to make us invisible to the cameras?"

"I'm trying to get us to the surface. To Mars. They can't bother us on Mars."

Sori had contacted the appropriate authorities on Mars and let them know a junior super-genius wanted to join them. He would participate in any endeavor they chose, he had offered, if they would just grant him one small concession: let him bring his mother and one of her friends.

"I'll need some on-the-job training," Sori said. "But I can achieve basic competence in almost any scientific specialty in three or four tendays. My current knowledge of mathematics and general science would probably be considered the equivalent of several doctorates in several widely varied fields. You'll like Mars, Joe. The accommodations aren't as luxurious as the accommodations on Phobos and Mercury, but most of the women are physically active, highly competent professionals. If you look back over your life, you'll find seventy percent of the women you've pursued meet that description."

Four hours after he started negotiating, he let me know everything was settled. We would make the descent in five hours. A bumper cargo vehicle was being outfitted with passenger couches.

"I felt we should leave as soon as we can," Sori argued. "A bumper may not be a luxury conveyance, but it's available."

"And how do I get to it without being disassembled by two of the larger residents of Phobos? I believe the embarkation lounge for descent vehicles is about ten kilometers from my front door."

A map of the local corridor system popped onto the screen. "There's an exit to the surface not too far from your apartment. You'll find a pressure suit waiting for you there. Take this elevator here just after you leave your apartment. Get off at this level and take this elevator here. We'll travel across the surface to a hatch that opens into the bumper's loading area."

"Have you ever used a pressure suit, Sori? Has your mother?"

"We're going to spend most of the next four hours working with the training simulation. I should have no trouble achieving proficiency between now and our embarkation time."

He was speaking very calmly and precisely, but I could see the glitter in his eyes. For him, it was the kind of adventure boys dream of. He was probably visualizing the way some of those "physically active, highly competent" professional women would react when he recounted his exploits.

My own visualizations were less buoyant. Sori had never been pursued—or caught.

But what else could I do? Return the money to Nento? Every time I thought of that, I responded with the same outrage I had felt when I had learned Nento was a manufactured lure. I couldn't escape from the emotional tangle she and her accomplices had created. I hated her because she had taken the emotion that has shaped my whole life and turned it against me. And I wanted her because she was a woman who had been trimmed and tuned until she fitted a template that matched some of my deepest longings.

I left my apartment a few minutes before the time Sori had given me. I sailed down the corridor as if I was aiming for an intersection on the far side of the elevator. I brushed the elevator button as I passed it and received the blessings of a minor miracle: the door opened just as I hit the floor. I threw myself at the elevator with my arms stretched in front of me and managed to grab the edge of the door before it started closing.

I was already slipping into pursuit panic when I stepped onto the floor where I was supposed to switch elevators. The new elevator was clearly marked *To Surface Exit*. The nearest surveillance camera was housed in a rotating ceiling mount about ten meters down the hall.

The donning room was a cheerless space a little bigger than the elevator. The exit had obviously been created for the benefit of people doing minor maintenance. The pressure suit was waiting for me on a shelf near the airlock, neatly folded into a square container. It had been manufactured by the same company that produced the last pressure suit I had worn. That had been almost thirty years ago, on the Moon, and a female killer had been pursuing me across the lunar regolith. The instructions that talked me through the donning procedure had been recorded by the same actress who had guided me through the process on the Moon.

The second container on the shelf confronted me with a novelty—a jet harness with propulsion tubes on each shoulder and eight maneuvering thrusters arranged around the straps. No one walks on the surface on a microgravity world like Phobos. I would skim across it at twelve kilometers per hour, gamely hoping my sessions with the simulator would help me avoid embarrassing end-over-end tumbles.

I exited into a field of solar panels. The top third of Mars' big red-orange disk loomed over my left horizon. The surface of Phobos was solid black in every direction—not *blackish*, or black *streaked*, but a real, undiluted *black*—and the glow from Mars created attractive effects. I clicked on the guidance program Sori had installed in the suit, and the famous actress started giving me instructions. I was supposed to line myself up with the yellow guidance arrow on the screen built into my right glove. I should keep moving in that direction until I passed the last row of panels and reached a large building with a lot of cables leading out of it.

The panel field ended just a few meters from the side of the building. It had been three decades since the first molecular machines had started transforming Phobos into a human habitat. By now, solar panels covered almost half the surface area. Most of the rest of the surface was cluttered with cable housings, recycling ducts, antennas, storage facilities, and all the other paraphernalia that keep civilization going. To someone who was born on Earth, places like Phobos look like inside-out cities. The people live inside and the surface contains all the things that are normally hidden under streets on Earth.

"You should wait here for the rest of your party," the suit said. "They should be here within five minutes. You should proceed without them if the wait exceeds twelve minutes."

I was early, they were late. I had been searching the horizon for a good ten minutes when I saw a silver suit and a red suit skim over a pair of tubes that dominated a rise about two hundred meters from the building. The silver suit was bigger than the red suit, so I assumed it contained Sori—a hypothesis that he confirmed by speeding ahead of his mother and executing a smooth series of S curves. He waved me on, and we converged on a route that paralleled another set of tubes.

Sori obviously mastered physical skills as easily as he conquered intellectual subjects. He was getting a lot of childish amusement out of the fact that he could assume almost any position he wanted to, once he propelled himself in the right direction. Once you're following the right trajectory on an airless microgravity world, you can rotate into any orientation that catches your fancy, as long as you maintain your height with a slight upward push from your thrusters. At one point, Sori managed to arrange himself so he was moving backward, with his feet pointed at the sky and his head aimed at the ground.

In spite of his tricks, Sori was keeping his fuel consumption to a minimum. His mother was another matter. Denava kept zigzagging across the course she was trying to follow. She would veer too far to one side, overcorrect, and veer too far the other way. Her orientation tended to be erratic, too. She kept overcorrecting her orientation in the same way she overcorrected her course deviations.

"It's a tricky skill," I radioed her. "Try keeping your bursts as short as possible. Don't be afraid to tumble some. It's the direction you're moving that counts, not the direction you're facing."

"You seem to have picked it up pretty fast. My showoff son said he thought you'd never done it before."

"I've had a lot of practice running away. I tend to be good at learning skills that can help me do it."

I grabbed her shoulder and applied a burst from my jet that helped her stabilize a right hand yaw. Her voice had sounded cool and totally unruffled. She really was a magnificent woman—warm, intelligent, collected. If it hadn't been for Nento, she and I would probably be sharing a quiet moment in some peaceful little corner. I had known I was sacrificing pleasure for turbulence when I had turned from her to Nento. Now I even knew my emotions had been manipulated by predators equipped with all the tools of modern psychology. And none of that knowledge gave me the slightest comfort. I was doing something I had never done in my life. I was denying the deepest impulses of my personality. I was running away from someone I should be moving toward.

The two muscle heads were both wearing black pressure suits. They should have taken us by surprise, given the color of Phobos' surface. Fortunately, they seemed to be just as inexperienced as we were. They came at us with the glow from Mars behind them, weaving around a long, badly calculated trajectory that gave us plenty of time to react.

We were still about twenty-five minutes from our goal. We couldn't outrun them with Denava slowing us down. They didn't even have to catch us. Once they realized we were trying to reach the hatch to the bumper vehicle, they could just race ahead of us and camp in front of our objective.

"I think we should split up," I said. "You go with your mother, Sori. Have you figured out how we should handle this?"

"Yes."

We broke to the right, on courses that differed by approximately twenty degrees. Denava wobbled into her son's legs as she tried to get on the right path, and Sori grabbed her harness with both hands. He fired a burst that compensated for her movements, and they sailed toward a trio of dish antennas.

The hoodlums did what I'd hoped they'd do. One veered toward me and the other raced after Sori and Denava. A thick stream of reaction mass spewed out of their jets.

The surface of Phobos is scarred by big grooves that look like they've been ploughed by grazing meteor strikes. I dropped over the rim of the first groove I came to, and fired a burst that brought me to a halt near the housing for an exit hatch.

My stalwart pursuer had used up a satisfactory quantity of fuel trying to catch up with me. Now he had to spew more fuel slowing down as he came over the top of the groove. I couldn't see his suit, but I could spot the white bursts from his jet.

They were very talkative boys. I had located the radio frequency they were using, and I could follow most of their activities merely by listening to them. I had been assuming Sori had come to the same conclusion I had, and I had apparently been right. He and his mother were hiding somewhere, too, and the muscle head pursuing them was circling the landscape in an attempt at a search pattern.

The key factor in the situation was the reaction mass left in our jets. Our pursuers had to use up fuel trying to overtake us when we ran away. They had to use up even more fuel looking for us when we hid. Sooner or later, they should run out.

The genius who was hunting me was kind enough to let out a yell when he finally took a close look at the hatch housing and realized the lump crouching beside it was the object of his quest. He gave me more useful help when he rushed straight at me with his jet releasing a long white plume. I cut away from him and glided toward a huge solar panel field while he reversed direction.

He had been going so fast he had to execute a wide curve to change direction. I slipped under the panels at the edge of the field and decided to take advantage of the fact that every panel was mounted on a thick upright. I cut my speed with the jet and started moving through the field on muscle power, heaving myself from upright to upright. The uprights were so lightly constructed I thought the first one I grabbed was going to bend. I lightened my touch and began covering ground without using fuel.

It was a sound economy measure, but it wasn't as clever as it looked. I didn't realize I was shaking a solar panel every time I wrapped my hand around an upright and pulled myself along. My esteemed adversary noticed my trail when I was somewhere in the middle of the field.

His howl of triumph knifed my eardrums. "I've got him! He's doing something that makes the panels quiver. I can follow the little lap toy just like he was leaving footprints!"

I've never understood why a man who enjoys the pleasures created by sexual differentiation should be considered less masculine than someone who spends his days adding extra bulk to his muscle tissue. Sexual union is, after all, the primary reason we're supposed to build up our strength and display our competitive prowess. Apparently, the male who wins a woman's favor by flexing his muscles is somehow superior to the "lap toy" who merely offers her a pleasant interlude.

I searched for him through the cracks between the panels, and spotted the glint of his helmet visor. He was holding station about a hundred meters up, where he could observe the whole field without moving. He had to fire his jet to maintain his altitude, but he could do that with a trickle of fuel consumption. He could have kept me pinned down for another hour.

I stopped swinging from panel to panel, and started working my way toward the edge of the panel field in a series of precise, carefully planned hops. With every hop, I had to take two factors into account: I couldn't touch a panel, and I had to stay close to the ground, so I wouldn't waste a lot of time coming down. If you drop a rock from shoulder height on Phobos, you'll spend twenty seconds watching it fall to the ground.

I turned on my jet as I emerged from the field, and we started another round of pressure-suit tag. He was a dangerous adversary, in spite of my low opinion of his intellectual capabilities. A pursuit in an airless, soundless environment is a nerve-wracking enterprise. It acquires extra grimness when your opponent happens to be wearing a black suit. The hound can be reaching for your throat before you know he's anywhere near you. He would have gotten me if he could have repressed his tendency to shout in triumph at the last minute. The fact that I was less massive helped me, too. For every second I held my jet open, I gained about sixty percent more speed than he did. I could change direction faster, too.

Sori adapted a more violent approach to his half of our problem. He let his man grab Denava, and closed in while the oaf tried to get his capture stabilized. Sori applied some kind of martial arts pain hold, and Denava followed her son's orders and held on. Their captive dragged them through a dizzying series of random maneuvers as he used up fuel struggling to break free. His super-strength arms shoved Denava away from him with a thrust that was so strong she had to waste fifteen seconds of fuel bringing herself to a stop.

They were almost two hundred meters above the surface when Sori's overgrown opponent started complaining he had run out of fuel. Sori checked the gauges on the poor fellow's jet harness to make sure it was true. Then he fired a burst from his own jet and put his helpless bundle on a trajectory that would bring it to a soft landing several kilometers from the bumper hatch.

I followed the struggle through the grunts and shouts coming through my earphones. It was a vivid demonstration of the problems I would have if I let my own pursuer get his hands on me.

My suit was keeping track of my fuel expenditure. Every five minutes, the voice of the famous actress advised me how much I had left. I was down to nineteen minutes, and I estimated my dance partner had been working his jet at least two minutes—or even three—for every minute I used mine. I could reach our objective with three minutes to spare, if my position indicator was correct. But he could probably reach it, too.

A familiar voice broke into the radio net. "What are you geniuses doing? Can't you see they're trying to make you use up your reaction mass? Haven't you realized they're obviously trying to reach the surface hatch for the bumper lounge? Quit playing children's games and get to the hatch before they do. They can't use the hatch if you're looming in front of it."

I had known Nento was an intelligent woman. The prescription for stimulating the romantic feelings of Joseph Louis Baske has always included liveliness, awareness, general competence, and all the other qualities a well-equipped head confers on the human personality. The people who think beauty is only a surface phenomenon have never understood the messages conveyed by the lines and movements of the female face. Until now, however, my perception of Nento's intelligence had been tempered by circumstance. Her imaginary business project had seemed dubious. She had responded to Sori's psychological manipulations as if she was incapable of skepticism.

Now her voice was crackling with competence. Now I was getting a glimpse of the woman who had planned the trap her trio had set for me. She and her accomplices had survived years of criminal activity. Her vocation might not favor people who possessed compassion and a refined sense of ethical behavior, but it tended to weed out the dull-witted and the weak-spirited.

My pursuer had been charging at me from the starboard side in his usual style. He swerved to the right and shot toward the bumper hatch with his jet churning out a stream that looked like it could push him all the way to the asteroid belt. Nento was urging him to watch his fuel consumption, but I discouraged that line of thought by blasting after him and drawing even with his left shoulder. He turned his helmet in my direction, and I underlined the message with an energy-wasting spurt that gave me a temporary hundred-meter lead. I gave him a snappy wave as I shot past him, and he rewarded me with a satisfying roar.

His safety mechanisms took over when he was a good two kilometers from the hatch. The jet stopped firing, and the thrusters cut his forward momentum as he settled toward the surface. I looked back as we drew apart and saw him settling into another cluster of solar panels. He was advising Nento he had run out of fuel, and she was telling him he should head for the hatch on foot as soon as he touched down.

My own reaction mass ran out when I was about four hundred meters from the hatch. I hit the surface with a slight lurch, just two hundred meters from safety, and started working my way through a tangle of cables and recycling tubes.

Nento grabbed me as I was jumping over a big pair of cables. She didn't say a word when she did it. I just felt something grab my harness and pull me almost straight up. She let me go after a few seconds, and I went up to a hundred meters and started to descend—a process that would take me almost two and a half minutes.

Her hands gripped my shoulders and turned me around. She had placed herself on the same trajectory. She backed off just out of arm's reach, and we floated down together.

It was one of the more embarrassing moments in a life which has included some illustrious examples of the genre. Without my jet, I was as helpless as a baby. She could shoot me back up when I got near the surface, and keep me rising and falling as long as she wanted to. And while I was bouncing up and down like a rubber doll, her large, very frustrated muscle boy was hopping across whatever obstacles the landscape put in front of him.

"I really find your behavior hard to believe, Joseph. I told you what the situation was. If they don't get their money out of you, they'll find some way to get it out of me. Is this the way you've treated all the women you claim you've loved?"

"You duped me," I said. "You redesigned yourself just so you could squeeze money out of me."

"Isn't that a little harsh? Didn't all those other women make a few changes here and there, too? What would we all look like if we didn't take advantage of the possibilities of modern medicine? Didn't you add a few centimeters to your height just recently?"

"It's not the same. That's normal behavior. You can't compare it with the scheme you set up. You took one of the best things evolution has given us and manipulated it for money. So you could add a few numbers to your bank account."

She stretched out her arm and ran her finger across the front of my helmet. "And why are you arguing with me, little Joe? Would you be arguing so hard if you were as angry as you say you are? Would you be engaging in such heated rhetoric if you didn't know you really want to give me everything you have to offer? In exchange for everything I can give you? Do you really want to run away to Mars and never know what you and I could have together? You're looking at the perfect woman, Joseph Louis—the woman shaped to fit your dreams. The woman you've been looking for all these decades. The woman none of the others *quite* were."

Sori had grasped the value of silence without being told—just as he seemed to understand all the tactical realities of our situation without being told. He swooped at me from behind Nento's back when we had fallen about eighty meters. He tackled me around the waist with his jet set at full power and started driving me toward the hatch. He even managed to sideswipe Nento and propel her into a tumble as he did it.

It was a nice try, but he was working with a serious handicap. Nento had just started using her jet. Sori had been optimizing his fuel consumption as if he had been working with a built-in computer program, but he had been forced to waste fuel stabilizing his mother and fighting it out with his half of the muscle twins. Nento stabilized herself before we had been traveling ten seconds. She grabbed me from the right side, with her arms stretched out, and started pushing us off course as if she was some kind of airborne tractor.

I closed my eyes. "Give it up, Sori. Get yourself and your mother out of this before you end up flopping around without any fuel, too."

"You're reacting with your emotions, Joe. I heard what she said. I'm not going to let you give in to her."

"You can't win. It's simple physics. She's got more fuel than you do."

He let go of me and activated a jet thrust that pushed him down a few meters. He shot straight up and drove his shoulder into Nento's stomach with a force that indicated he had never developed any inhibitions about the damage he could inflict on the female body. They bounced away from each other—action and reaction—but Nento retained her grip on my jet harness.

I was giving Sori the kind of advice the young should receive from their elders. He would obviously be a lot happier on Mars than I would. Did he really think his mother would enjoy seeing him battered into unconsciousness and left lying on the surface with a few well-placed gaps in his bone structure?

But I knew he was right, too. My mind was already toying with the possibilities Nento had raised. I didn't think our time together would turn into a permanent liaison, in spite of the hold she had on me. But suppose it did go on for a while? I would start by giving back the money I had taken from her—freely, as a gift. Then I could feed her more money from time to time, to keep her coming back.

I could visualize the whole interlude. I could see everything we would do together, from the moments when I would hold all that naked loveliness pressed against me to the small, mundane activities that glow like jewelry when you do them with a woman who excites cravings that permeate your entire personality. Did it really matter how much money she eased out of my bank account? Hadn't I always claimed I had spent my life enjoying something that was worth almost any sum? Nento and her partners had enmeshed me in their trap because they had offered me something priceless—a woman who had been deliberately endowed with the attributes that would give me the greatest pleasure and evoke the most powerful responses.

I couldn't twist myself around without help, but I could lower my left hand and grab Nento's right forearm. I could pull myself around, once I had a purchase on her, and wrap my fingers around her other arm.

There were a number of things Sori could do once I had her hands immobilized. He could have smashed her hard in the head, for example, and knocked her unconscious. He chose one of the simplest and most elegant alternatives. He maneuvered underneath her and unlatched the two buckles that held her jet harness in place.

She activated the jet and tried to pull away from him, but we both held on. The harness was designed for a quick release in emergencies. Sori ripped it off her suit and pushed her into a vertical trajectory that looked like it would keep her aloft for at least five minutes. He launched himself at me as soon as he let her go, and we shot across the three hundred meters that separated us from his mother and the hatch to the bumper lounge.

We reached the lounge just three or four minutes before they closed the boarding gate, which was a blessing in the circumstances. By the time Nento managed to land and cross the surface, I was safely strapped into my couch and all the hatches on the lander had been sealed.

"I knew you wouldn't let her lure you back," Sori pontificated. "Your personality structure includes a strong autonomy vector, Joe. You never mention it when you describe yourself, but it's there, even if you aren't aware of it. It probably has more influence on your behavior patterns than you think. It's obvious women exert a strong effect on you. But that isn't the only reason you never form a long-term bond."

A descent in a bumper lander is just as dull and terrifying as most rides in space vehicles. You lie on your back in a windowless, grimly functional closet, and hope everything works when it's supposed to.

First you wonder if the heat shield will survive the initial contact with the atmosphere. Then you wonder if the parachutes are going to open. (I even wondered if the parachutes really *had* opened, in spite of the lander's reassurances. Isn't it possible the program would lie to you, so you wouldn't scream too much as you fell to your death?) The wait for the news that the retrorockets have fired adds a little more tension.

The big exception to the standard routine of boredom and apprehension is the airbag landing. We bounced five times altogether, and we were all laughing and making whooping sounds by the time we started down for the second bounce. A Mars bumper lander is the biggest trampoline the human race has built to date. The parachutes and the retrorockets do their part, but a drop of ten thousand kilometers still gives you an eminently satisfactory set of bounces.

I had left my personal fabricator on Phobos, but I had brought copies of all the fabrication programs I had purchased over the last thirty years. That night we toasted our success with the best champagne on the menu. There was a little awkwardness over the sleeping arrangements, as you would expect. Sori had told the Martians his mother and I had a domestic arrangement, and they had given him a two-bedroom suite. I manfully announced I would camp out in the living room, but I was voted down. Sori had already started stuffing the living room with equipment and turning it into a major office facility. He would be doing a lot of in-person entertaining and consulting. I would obviously be in the way if I tried to use his office as a bedroom.

Denava and I shared the second bedroom as roommates. It was an uncomfortable arrangement, but we could both see the humor in it. We both wanted the thing we had started and never finished. We both kept hoping it would start again. But we both wanted the real thing. Neither one of us wanted to pretend.

Nento phoned me several times during the next couple of tendays. Sori had placed a block on her calls, so I wasn't even aware she was still interested. Four tendays after we arrived on Mars, Sori told me he thought I should call her.

"Do you really think that's wise, doctor?" I said.

"Trust me, my son."

The woman who answered the phone had a softer, rounder face, like the original Nento I had seen in the pictures Sori had shown me. She had thinner lips than the Nento in the picture, and her hair had been gathered into a braid that hung down her back. She still used the sideward look, but she lowered her head when she did it. She spoke in short, slow phrases, and her voice never rose above a murmur.

She wasn't the Nento who had attracted me, and she wasn't the original Nento, either. She insisted she was still thinking about me, but it was obvious she was just reciting lines.

"They've remodeled her again," Sori said. "I guess they decided it could be a profitable technique, even if it didn't work with you. Most of their victims won't have somebody like me hovering in the background."

Can you mourn for someone who never existed? I was sharing a bedroom with a woman who possessed almost all the qualities Nento had pretended to have, and I still found myself moping around like I'd lost everything I'd ever wanted.

"It's ridiculous," I said. "I haven't lost a thing. She never was. And yet she's got a stronger hold on me than half the real women I've been in love with."

"Feelings are feelings," Denava said. "You've spent your life obeying an irrational impulse. It's part of your charm."

"I can't believe I'm spending my life running from woman to woman just because none of them matches some ideal I'm stuck with. That isn't it. That's never been it."

"So what are you doing?"

"It's the variety that fascinates me. You're all different. Every one of you."

"So sooner or later, you'd have grown tired of her, too."

"Sooner or later someone else *attracts* me. It isn't the same thing."

Denava had opted for the cello when she had installed her performance system. I spent a little money and bought a program that reproduced one of Amati's finest. It was a perfect companion for the new copy of my Amati violin that I ran off soon after we settled into our quarters. We played together for two or three hours every day. We even got in some ensemble playing with the half dozen Martians who felt they could indulge in such activities. Eventually—inevitably—there came a day when I looked at her across the strings of my instrument and we both knew her grave, controlled personality had once again touched my flightier temperament.

We spent over two Eyears together. A full Martian year. Then the dance of life spun me toward a biological designer who was working with the faction that was planning the terraforming of Mars, if terraforming ever became the approved policy. The biological designer was followed by a physiological psychologist, the psychologist was followed by a life support engineer, and Sori's prophecy proved to be true. Mars was a very pleasant world for someone with my disposition.

Still, I left it after seven Eyears. For all its pleasures, it had a flaw that troubled my happiest hours. On all the worlds where people live underground, the public spaces are decorated with panoramic screens that show you the landscape you would see if you were looking through a real window. In every cafe and public area on Mars, day or night, you can contemplate the Martian hills and the Martian sky. Three times a day, if you happen to be near a screen at the right time, you can see an astronomical object which orbits the planet every 7.7 hours, at a distance of ten thousand kilometers. It's a small object, and not very bright. But I never learned to ignore it.

ROMANCE FOR AUGMENTED TRIO

Now it is impossible to judge of equality, whether physical or moral, except by appearances; from which it follows that the citizen who wants to avoid persecution must, if he is not like everyone else or worse, bend his every effort to appearing to be so. If he has much talent, he must hide it; if he is ambitious, he must pretend to scorn honors; if he wants to obtain anything, he must ask for nothing; if his person is handsome, he must neglect it; he must look slovenly and dress badly, his accessories must be of the plainest, he must ridicule everything foreign; he must bow awkwardly, not pride himself on being well mannered, care little for the fine arts, conceal his good taste if he has it; not have a foreign cook; he must wear an ill-combed wig and be a little dirty.
 —Giacomo Casanova, *History of My Life*, tr. Willard R. Trask

I knew there was something wrong as soon as I took my eyes off Ganmei's face and looked at her clothes. She was wearing the loose shirt-and-shorts combination she usually wore when she went about her everyday business on the ship. In the past, she had always put on something special when she had activated my baseline personality—my normal personality as my old-fashioned brain still thought of it. The last time she had brought me back she had been wearing a black form-fitting gown that sheathed her in the glitter of the High Cold War period.

I stared at her while her litany of disaster flowed across my brain. Our ship had been taken over… twenty robots of unknown origin now occupied the outside of the hull… the robot invaders had destroyed every long-range antenna on the hull… it had been almost three tendays since she had received any incoming messages… or sent any messages out.

It was a disorienting moment. Ganmei had started firing information at me as soon as she had turned off the music-obsessed secondary personality I had chosen when we had left the asteroid belt six years earlier. One minute I had been standing in my music bower, completely absorbed in my interactions with the shadows who were playing the flute and harp parts in Claude Debussy's sonata for flute, viola, and harp. Then I had heard Ganmei's voice repeating the trigger words over the intercom, and all the feelings she aroused had flooded through my consciousness.

She waved her hand at the wheeled boxes positioned near an emergency hatch. "I've fabricated forty-two armed robots. They're standing by all over the ship. I'm going to launch an attack as soon as we get settled into the control room."

She studied my face. "You do understand, don't you? I'm not going too fast for you?"

I shook my head. "The only problem I'm having now is a perfectly reasonable difficulty adjusting my emotions. I had assumed you returned me to my baseline state so we could enjoy another few days together. It's been almost twelve tendays since our last interlude. Instead, I'm listening to you tell me we've become the captives of some mysterious aggressor. I take it you thought I'd be better off if I went on fiddling while you prepared to wage war."

"I felt I had to bring you back to baseline before I actually started the combat phase. You obviously have to be functioning at your optimal level if anything goes wrong. But I didn't see any point in bringing you back earlier."

We had been talking in a high-speed synthetic language called CM—a Latin-based, very compressed language the members of Ganmei's genetic cohort had developed for their own use. Ganmei had developed a learning program and an auxiliary intelligence file especially for me, and I had gritted my teeth and applied myself. We used CM whenever we were discussing practical matters or anything that didn't require a lot of emotional communication. Now she rested her hand on my shoulder and switched to ordinary, day-to-day Techno-Mandarin.

"I'm sorry if it was the wrong thing to do. It was a hard judgment to make. I could have used some company."

She really was a magnificent creature. You couldn't spend an hour with her without realizing that big leaps in intelligence affected the entire human personality. She was still only in her forties, but she had mapped out most of my emotional makeup before we had spent two tendays together. Her fingers were pressing on my shoulder with a grip that managed to be comradely and suggestive at the same time.

Her parents had opted for gracefulness rather than strength and endurance when they had planned her. She had spent most of her childhood in the asteroid belt, but she had been born on Earth and she had a rangy sturdiness that reflected the influence of both her youthful environments. She was a head taller than me, in spite of the extra length I had added to my legs. A lot of the women I've courted have lived a little closer to the ceiling than I do. My lack of height can be an advantage. I don't make them feel dominated or overpowered.

Her intelligence and her physical attributes were an important part of her appeal. I wouldn't have sought her out if she hadn't possessed them. But they weren't the primary reason I had decided to spend fifteen years of my life span on a trip to the outer edge of the solar system. She had beguiled me before I had even seen her picture. I had been exploring the databanks, and I had stumbled on an interview transcript in which she had described her Kuiper Belt project.

It would take forty years to reach the Kuiper Belt if you used a minimum energy trajectory, Ganmei had told the interviewer. *And another forty years to get back. I'm going to get there in five. When I reach the Belt, I'll have just enough reaction mass left to match orbits with a* suitable Kuiper Object—preferably a large object that's made entirely of water ice. I'll take on the water as reaction mass and spend two or three years in the belt, fabricating the telescope array out of the materials I'll find there. Then I'll attach the ship to another suitable object and head for home. The second object will give me so much reaction mass that I'll make the homebound trip in three years and still be able to brake when I approach the asteroids.

So your whole plan depends on your ability to use the material in the Kuiper Belt?

That's what makes it a viable project—something I can handle all by myself. I'm a little surprised I'm the only person who's thought of it. It seems like such an obvious idea.

You're telling me you're going to play games with multi-megaton objects. And you feel that's obvious?

Most of the women I've loved have been exceptionally intelligent. Many have been graceful (though a certain vulnerable clumsiness has its charms, too). Ganmei had audacity and imagination. She had conceived the entire project on her own. She had built her ship with almost no help. She had plowed through the international bureaucracies that authorize the private use of nuclear material. She would have made the whole trip by herself if I hadn't come along and offered her a more humane possibility.

I wasn't surprised she had decided she should leave me in my private musical world and deal with a mysterious military assault by herself. I could have complained, but why resist the effects of the hand fondling my shoulder?

"Have you received any messages from the people behind this?" I said. "Have they given you any idea what they want?"

"I've received four messages from the Voice of a ship. It claims it's relaying the words of its 'organic colleague.' Here's the first one."

She gave our ship an order, and a picture of the exterior of our hull appeared on a wall screen. The camera zoomed in and settled on three wheeled vehicles. A Voice boomed out of a loudspeaker.

I covered my ears. "Is it always that loud?"

"Always."

The Voice sounded harsher and more masculine than the Voices of most of the machines I've listened to over the years. It was advising Ganmei our ship was now under its control.

"Your communications outlets and your thrusters have all been destroyed," the Voice proclaimed. "The machines that have occupied your surface area are now installing a new thruster system—a system I and my organic colleague will control. Your ship is now a prison. You and your peculiar companion are now its prisoners in residence."

"It just happened," Ganmei said. "All at once. Suddenly I had no contact with the world outside the ship. Then I received that message. I tried to send answers over our internal communications system. I asked them what they wanted. I didn't hear a thing for five more days."

She gave our own Voice another order, and I listened while it played the other three messages. In the third message, the other Voice let us know we could be imprisoned in our ship for decades. In the fourth, it said we would be here as long as its organic colleague wanted to hold us captive.

I lowered my head and thought. I had learned to take my time when I discussed anything important with Ganmei. It was a little like a handicap in a game—I got to use ten units of time for every unit she devoted to the conversation. I was consuming the best intelligence enhancers anyone had been able to design for me, but she still made me feel like a plodding adolescent trying to dance with a star ballerina.

"Did you make them any offers? Money? Sex?"

"I just asked them what they wanted. I started fabricating my own army right after I got the first message. I responded to the Voice primarily because I was afraid they might realize I was preparing a counter-attack if I didn't make some attempt to negotiate with them. I thought I might gain some information. But so far I haven't heard anything that sounded particularly useful."

I looked around the room. I had spent six years on the ship without feeling restricted or confined. Ganmei had a good eye. The greenery she had chosen surrounded us with life and complexity. She had interwoven eight different species when she had arranged the vines that covered the ceiling. The floor plants bloomed in a complicated mix of cycles that created an unpredictable medley of moods and colors.

"You're feeling it, too," Ganmei said.

"All at once—it's a cage. A cell. Even with you here."

"We can't stay out here forever. I might make it through another three or four decades without a major medical problem. At your age—even in the condition you're in—you probably can't go more than twenty years without developing a problem that requires the services of a major medical complex."

"You must have used up a lot of our materials fabricating the new robots."

"I recycled most of the robots I've been using on the telescopes along with a lot of our exercise equipment. I'm afraid we're going to be short on amenities. I'm hoping I'll be able to refabricate the work robots once we break free. But I decided it was silly to worry about that now. Our first priority is to break free."

I nodded. I could think of objections to the whole idea of an all-out mechanized brawl. What would she do, for example, if she cleared the enemy from our ship, and our mysterious captor responded with another force that was just as large as the first?

"You're ready to attack now?" I asked.

"Everything is in place. I'm ready to start as soon as you feel you can handle the stress."

"Then let's go."

How could I argue with her? Her basic, unenhanced brain was supposed to be five times better than the fully enhanced, late-20th Century model housed in my skull. And I had received ample proof it really was.

We took the elevator to the control room. Ganmei strapped herself into the pilot's couch and I settled into the spectator/minor-assistant couch she had added to the plans when she had decided fifteen years of celibacy might, after all, be a trifle tedious.

My secondary personality had been Ganmei's idea. I could have spent long periods in induced hibernation, but that would have required some maintenance work on her part.

I was supposed to spend approximately two years as my charming, irresistibly enamored self. That was about the length of time my longest love affairs had lasted. Every few tendays, as her schedule (and her inclinations) allowed it, Ganmei would reactivate my baseline personality, and we would enjoy a romantic idyll. My memories of the times we had spent together over the last six years were an uninterrupted series of dinners, long talks, and sexual interludes that were a feast of tenderness, good humor, and sensuality. The rest of the time, I had stayed in my own quarters, out of her way, and my secondary personality had happily spent its days poring over scores and working its way through the violin literature of the 19th and 20th Centuries.

It had been Ganmei who had suggested I switch musical periods. I had installed a performance system in my nervous system back in the 2030s, when I had fallen in love with a woman who spent all her leisure hours playing Baroque music on the flute. I had taken up the short-necked Baroque violin so I could join her social circle. For most of the next hundred years, I had reveled in 18th Century music—especially the music of Bach. Ganmei had felt my secondary might be happier exploring something new, and she had been right. The switch to the longer-necked 19th Century violin had only required a minor adjustment in the information molecules I had implanted during my last upgrade. I could even play the viola—and lose myself in Debussy's wonderful exercise in tone color and musical complexity.

"Would you like me to run through the overall battle plan?" Ganmei asked.

"I think I'd just as soon get started."

"I've been war-gaming it every moment I've had. There are usually some moments when it looks like our side is done for."

"I'll keep that in mind."

A schematic of our ship appeared on my screen. Red symbols showed me where her electronic warriors would pour out of the hatches. Five of the symbols were located on the wheel. The sixth was just behind us, in the part of the hub that separated the control room from the nuclear pile.

The wheel on the screen was turning at the same rate the real wheel turned. Near the bottom of the rim, I could make out the location of the bower where I had been playing Debussy just a few minutes before. The six squads were supposed to erupt from their hatches simultaneously. The individual robots were all equipped with gripping devices, so they could maneuver on the tubes that connected the wheel to the hub.

Ganmei had settled into a high-powered external brain-machine interface. Her face had disappeared behind a featureless black visor. Molded red ceramic covered the rest of her head.

Red symbols flowed out of the six hatches on my schematic. Yellow symbols marked the positions of the enemy machines as the sensors on our robots picked them up. Three of the hatches were small openings designed for single-person emergency exits. Our robots had to squeeze through those hatches two at a time. It looked to me like the enemy was responding with a fast buildup in front of each hatch.

Something happened I didn't understand. Somehow one of our squads broke through its opposition. It spread out behind the enemy, and the table on top of my screen added six enemy machines to its "destroyed" tally. I glanced at Ganmei, but the only emotional signal I could pick up was the tension in her hands as she gripped the arms of her couch.

After that, the battle spread over the entire surface of the ship. None of it made any tactical sense to me. There were times when I thought I understood a small skirmish. Then one of the robots would suddenly lurch off in an unexpected direction or break off combat just when I thought it was about to score. And I would stare at the screen and wonder what had happened.

I had once spent a few tendays pretending I was seriously interested in learning to play Go. Now I felt like I was watching two grandmasters. Ganmei and her opponent could consider the obvious thoughts my brain produced, calculate the other player's best counter-move, and come up with combinations that would thwart possibilities I couldn't follow even if they were explained to me step by step. The only aspect of the situation I could grasp was the numbers that tallied the losses. Two hours after the battle started, Ganmei had destroyed sixteen of the enemy's robots and lost twenty of hers. By the end of the third hour, the score was eighteen to twenty-five in her opponent's favor.

She spent the last thirty minutes guiding two robots through a desperate game of hide and seek, shooting from ambush as she tried to destroy a few more enemy machines before her own machines joined the final casualty list. The Voice of the enemy ship boomed through our loudspeakers seconds after her last robot fired its last projectile.

"You have once again demonstrated the futility of genetically enhanced intelligence. You have been contending with a machine that is infinitely superior to the limited organ you carry in your skull. Your existence is based on an arrogant fallacy. The future belongs to machine brains guided by human minds. The best genetically enhanced brains will always be inferior to the best machines. Your arrogance has led you into an evolutionary dead end. The lessons of history teach us…"

This time the message ran on for almost twenty minutes. I would have turned it off long before it ended, but I knew rants like that could provide you with useful clues to the personality behind them. This one contained fourteen repetitions of the word "arrogant."

Ganmei didn't raise her visor until the harangue finally came to a stop. Her head slumped forward as soon as I removed the interface from her hands.

Giacomo Casanova's escape from an infamous Venetian prison is one of the best-told adventure stories in the databanks. He turned it into a best-selling book years before he wrote his memoirs and recounted it at salons all over Paris, in return for dinner and an entrée into the upper levels of Parisian society. It's a good story, but I felt his imprisonment was the most heart-wrenching episode in his memoirs. He had escaped after fifteen months, but he could have been caged in his cell for half a decade, at a time when he was still in his twenties. What would years of imprisonment have done to a man of his temperament, at that period of his life?

I would have Ganmei, of course. I wouldn't be womanless. But how would I feel about her as the years dragged on? How would she feel about me? My life had been a dance that whirled me from one partner to another. From the time I had been seven years old, I had been immersed in an unbroken succession of faces, touches, enchantments, and longings. What would I do if the dance suddenly stopped?

My secondary personality wouldn't offer me a satisfactory hiding place. Up to now, it had been an innocuous way to pass the time between pleasant interludes. Now it would be an escape from an intolerable situation. I would feel like I was committing suicide every time I activated it.

We returned to the wheel and dropped onto a couch in Ganmei's quarters. We spent most of the next hour sitting side by side, fitfully holding hands.

Sori Dali had given me some insights into the psychology of sexual criminals when he had helped me escape the trap Nento and her colleagues had constructed for me on Phobos. The ideas crowding his hyper-active brain generated an irresistible pressure to talk. We had concentrated on the psychology of swindlers, but Sori knew I would be interested in the male-female aspects of his researches. Our unknown captor seemed to fit the standard model for serial killers and serial rapists that Sori had presented me. He seemed to be primarily interested in domination and control—not sex or money or any of the other bonbons he could have demanded. Historically, criminals like that tended to be men who felt inferior or socially rejected. They struck at women who had superior status—women who would normally ignore them.

Ganmei obviously met the victim criteria. The "organic colleague," on the other hand, had just defeated her in a head-to-head clash of intellects. He had assembled a ship that was just as good as Ganmei's, and followed her to the outer reaches of the Solar System. You could even argue that he had overcome more obstacles than Ganmei, when you took into account the illegal aspects of his activities. Ganmei was the only person in the databanks who had ever received legal permission to use nuclear material to fuel an expedition to the Kuiper Belt.

He had done all that, however, with the help of a brain-machine interface. Every message he had transmitted had indicated he couldn't compete with her without the help he received from his Voice.

It had been over forty years since I had parted with Ling Chime on Mercury, but she was still the first person I thought of when I let myself ponder the disruptions created by the biological developments in biotechnology that had altered the basic structure of the human race in the last century. If someone like Ling could retreat into a tepid, emotional backwater, convinced she was merely a trial version of the people who were going to "replace" her, why couldn't there be a few males whose anger would drive them across the orbits of every planet in the Solar System?

The human race was struggling through another period of turmoil and adjustment. The advances in medicine that had taken place during the 21st Century had given us life spans that could encompass centuries. Any disease could be cured. Any defect could be ameliorated. Yet, at the same time, the biological wizards had created a world in which we could spend all those centuries in the company of people who possessed intellectual and physical powers that made us look like primitive, 20th Century versions of the latest software.

I started talking primarily because I knew we had to start working our way back to a functional mood. Unfortunately, Ganmei immediately perceived the obvious corollary to my theoretical ramblings. "You're describing someone who could be very difficult to deal with, Joe. If you're right—if he's only interested in dominating and controlling me—then I don't have anything to bargain with. He's already got everything he wants."

Her voice sounded as distant—and weak—as the sun looked when I viewed it on one of our screens. Ganmei was a mature woman by the standards of the world that had shaped my childhood, but she had been sheltered from some of the rougher realities of human behavior. She had spent most of her life with her own kind. Her parents had bought her the best brain on the market and cultivated her potential with a full-time post-natal environment that had surrounded her with "intellectually stimulating experiences" and "cognitively challenging peers." Her sexual partners had all been young men who were her intellectual equals. Her relationships with them had been pleasant, but emotionally mild. Then she had become absorbed in the construction of her ship and her preparations for her big project. This was the first time she had confronted the psychological disasters that could bedevil people who had been formed by the random workings of genetics and childhood experience.

"I was just giving you the benefit of my knowledge," I said. "I have the utmost confidence in your ability to put it to good use."

She twisted around on the couch. Her fingers slid along the side of my face. "I think it's time we both shut off our brains for awhile. And I took advantage of your vast experience in other areas. Do you think you can do that? I'll start looking for a new approach tomorrow. I promise."

I didn't think someone like Ganmei could shut off her brain. But everybody reaches an emotional limit sooner or later. For the next thirty minutes, she managed to produce a convincing simulation of a warm, mammalian lump. She dropped off to sleep as soon as I slipped off her. She didn't wake up for almost half a day cycle.

Ganmei started working on a new escape program as soon as she consumed one of the enormous breakfasts she seemed to require. Our problem could be divided into two phases, she announced. First, she had to maneuver our captor into a face-to-face meeting. Then she had to get him under control.

The second phase, she decided, could be handled in her laboratory, where she would develop a new class of molecular machines. We had to assume our enemy would subject us to a thorough skin search if he ever let us enter his presence. She would evade his detectors with an anti-personnel mole that could be broken into six subunits. She would carry three subunits on each hand, and they would recombine when she brought them together on his body.

"State of the art detection systems can detect combinations that are constructed from four subunits," Ganmei advised me. "No one, as far as I know, has ever made the jump to six-unit combinations. The big problem will be the time it takes them to assemble. I'm going to have to make an effort if I'm going to get that down to something reasonable."

It was exacting work. It demanded a lot of testing and retesting. I could help her with some of it but I couldn't really follow it.

The other phase of her schemes would have been relatively simple if we'd had access to all the psychological material available in the public databanks. Criminal personalities tend to be relatively uncomplicated. We would have constructed a personality model in which we had some confidence, and she would have tested approaches until she found something she could apply without worrying it might be counter-productive.

The information stored in our onboard databanks merely reinforced the general picture I had already sketched in. We spent most of our time analyzing the rants she had received and the messages she had tried to send back. He hadn't answered her messages, but that was information in itself. We knew his robots could pick up our messages if he was listening. Our ship's internal communication system could reach the area around the hull. She hadn't received an answer because he hadn't responded.

My major contribution was a suggestion that helped us move the modeling project off ground zero. "We've gotten everything we're going to get out of a model for the time being," I said. "Why don't we use some common sense? If there's a real live male on the other ship—and any human who does something like this is almost certainly male—then we know two things about him. He's been alone for over five years. And he's been womanless. Why don't you ask him some questions about himself? Why he's doing this? What kind of music he likes? Anything to get him talking."

She went back to her lab, and I whiled away my time planning dinner. She had used up a lot of our raw materials building her robot army, but the fabricators could still turn out decent wines. I had loaded my entire library of wine programs into our databanks before we left, in spite of Ganmei's belief that a small selection would be sufficient. She came out of the lab an hour after she left me, and I listened while she recited the message she had composed while she had been working on her moles.

She had decided to ask him how he had managed to build his ship in complete secrecy all by himself. She would raise the subject, she said, with a nicely calculated combination of awe mingled with a hint of disbelief. Her words had been chosen with some care, but she let her tone of voice carry most of the emotional content—the suggestion she was becoming fascinated by the cunning, mysterious being who had taken her captive and defeated her in combat.

We went over the message until we both felt she had struck the right balance between submissiveness and simple adventurer-to-adventurer curiosity. "I don't think you should make it too obvious," I said. "Let his imagination do some of the work."

His answer didn't reveal too many details. Mostly it was a long boast, with the Voice of his ship couching the whole diatribe in "my colleague feels" statements. But that was good enough. We had started a dialogue.

And once he'd started, he kept on—just as I'd hoped. He knew we were gathering information for a personality model. He even told us we should make sure we put certain facts into the model. We should note, he said, that he was the son of a demanding and possessive mother and a father who had disappeared before his third birthday. But he still couldn't stop talking. And the more he talked, the more Ganmei refined her approach.

She kept commenting on how trivial it all looked. "Every time I look at that model," she said, "I want to reach inside and make a few alterations. Adjust a couple of chemical pathways. Make some changes in his relationship with his mother. It all seems so *unnecessary*."

I had been born into a world in which children were molded by parental whims and biochemical accidents. To Ganmei, an environment like that seemed unimaginably primitive. With the psychological techniques we had developed over the last century, there was no reason why anyone should have to live with the kind of personality distortions displayed in our model. Most of the children born in the last fifty years had probably been endowed with parents who gave them the advantages that produced adults like her.

But most isn't all. We were still living in a society that was infinitely rougher and more chaotic than Ganmei's childhood milieu. Every year, thousands of children were still being brought into the world by parents who were irresponsible, or domineering, or just plain incompetent. If you added in all the people, like me, who had been born before the development of personality development techniques, you had to conclude that most of the people living in the Solar System had been shaped by the forces that had buffeted developing personalities since the dawn of consciousness. We pre-scientific versions of humanity might have trouble living with Ganmei and her colleagues—but they were going to spend a long time living with *us*.

Up until now, I had seen Ganmei primarily during her recreational hours. I had agreed to that, but it had left a big hole in our relationship. Now I felt I had truly made contact. I could listen to her while she explained her problems. I could feel the intellectual intensity she focused on the messages she composed. I gave her suggestions whenever I thought it might be helpful, and watched her twirl my ideas around and transform two or three into approaches she could use.

Our recreational time took a different turn, too. We spent hours playing Bach together. On her own, Ganmei normally played music written in the last thirty years by genetically enhanced composers. Most of it seemed formless and fragmented to my mind, but I could understand why. For people with her kind of brain it was a compressed musical language in which a few notes could be loaded with implications. When she turned to the music of the past, she usually played the scholarly literature written for the classic Chinese qin. Bach had produced the one body of work we could both relate to. His music had enough complexity to keep her interested, and it was part of a tradition I had been exploring for over a century.

Ganmei had never purchased a performance system. She had taught herself to play the qin and all the standard keyboard instruments, without any help from implants. She played the harpsichord when we played Bach together—a small, beautifully constructed instrument I had selected for her when she had decided she could let me share her adventure. She usually chose the harpsichord when she sat by herself playing the music created by her intellectual equals.

When he finally did what we wanted, he couched it as an order—just as our model had predicted he would. Ganmei would report to his ship at once, he proclaimed. She resisted, naturally—and gave herself time to finish working on her moles.

She had originally planned to confront him by herself. I pointed out that I had more experience with violent situations, but she dismissed that argument out of hand. So I appealed to her concern for my welfare.

"What if he keeps you with him and abandons me? I'll be here all by myself. For decades. Maybe for the rest of my life."

"Without a female companion."

"Yes."

He laughed at her when she told him she wanted to bring me with her. Once again, I had to listen to rants in which I was referred to as an "erotic convenience."

By this time, we had a model we thought we could trust. Ganmei displayed it on an oversize screen and scanned it while she assailed him with a series of pleadings, cajolings, and coquettish attacks of stubbornness. She responded to every subtle variation in the vectors and symbols on the model screen as if she were steering a high-speed vehicle through a particularly treacherous obstacle course. The real personality responded just like the model. And finally, after one last fifteen-minute harangue, generously announced that he was going to let me accompany my "controller."

I had done a little arguing myself, and Ganmei had modified her original plan. I wasn't going to be defenseless. She had outfitted my hands with six-unit moles that could damage robots and other metal objects.

"I'd let you have anti-personnel moles," she had said apologetically. "But I didn't have time to come up with a completely different design that would do the same job. His security system might notice if it found the same unusual molecular fragments on both of us. This will be the only chance we'll have, Joe. We have to keep every risk to a minimum."

She had paid some attention to our communication implants, too. We wouldn't be able to relay through the communication system on the other ship, so she gave us a big increase in range—along with some carefully phrased instructions. "You'll feel the drain on your energy if you use the enhanced implant more than a few minutes. I'm going to upgrade your encryption program and modify the transmission program so it automatically crams everything into blips, but you shouldn't transmit any messages unless it's absolutely necessary. The blips and the encryption will slow up his cryptography system, but his Voice will probably break the encryption minutes after it intercepts our first message. I'd be happier if you stayed off the air until you received something from me."

She was speaking very matter-of-factly, but I still picked up the undertones. She was going to bring me with her, but I was supposed to shut up and follow her instructions.

I smiled. "Is the communication package going to include some kind of anesthetic? So you can put me to sleep if I start doing something really stupid?"

"I thought about it."

She shrugged as she said it—a gesture that was just as winning as everything else she did. Then she put her hand on my shoulder.

"I just want to make sure I can keep us coordinated. We're dealing with someone who's already demonstrated he can defeat me. I can't forget that. He may be a mess psychologically. But he's still a match for me intellectually when he's working with his Voice."

I told her she could modify my implants in any way she wanted, of course. But I knew she felt uncomfortable. So I engaged in a little manipulation of my own and broached a contingency plan I had been pondering. If she couldn't get him under control, I suggested, I could try to reach the emergency communications system in his control room. The emergency system in a spacecraft is always set up so it operates outside the main computer system. If I could reach it, I could send a message to two of the brightest people I had ever known: Ling Chime and the young man, Sori Dali, who had briefed me on criminal psychology. I would tell them our situation and ask them to radio a computer virus to his ship. They both had the ability to design something that could slip past the best state-of-the-art security system.

Ganmei accepted the idea as soon as I suggested it, but she let me know she had reservations. "It's something we should try only if we're really desperate, Joe. The time lag alone could invalidate the whole idea. Even if you actually managed to get a message out, it would be five or six hours before it reaches either of them. Ten hours *minimum* before we receive a reply. If you add in the time it would take to create a virus—it might be two or three day cycles."

She believed me, however, when I told her I thought both of them would respond. "I might have thought you were crazy if I hadn't spent so much time with you," she said. "You're telling me you feel you can rely on a woman you were in love with over thirty years ago. And the son of a woman you were in love with just a few years later. And I haven't got the slightest doubt you probably can."

There were a number of women who wouldn't want to hear from me again. But it was nice to know she understood the friendly ones. We'd had some good times together—some of the best I'd ever had.

This was the first time I had floated across several kilometers of open space in a pressure suit. There were moments when the grandeur of the scene managed to overwhelm the queasy sensations that troubled my stomach. At one point, I could actually see both ships at the same time, with their wheels majestically revolving around the long hubs that contained their control rooms and their propulsion units. Off to my right, there was a white disc that was a little bigger than my glove—the only natural object I could detect in all that emptiness. The Kuiper Belt may contain thousands of iceballs and planetoids, but it's just like the asteroid belt—when you're in it, the space around you normally looks empty.

The shipboard robots that met us at the airlock were built around a standard wheeled box that carried a few more arms and sensor poles than Ganmei's shipboard machines. It wasn't hard to spot the arms that housed their mole projectors. They remained fixed on us from the moment we squeezed through the hatch.

Our captor was sitting in a chair that had a high, thronelike back. He was—not unexpectedly—a pudgy man who should have spent more time with his exercise equipment. He was wearing a golden robe and—so help me!—red boots.

Two robots shepherded us to a spot directly in front of his chair. I caught a whiff of the scent he was wearing. His hair and his stubby blonde beard both looked as if they had been trimmed just a few minutes before we boarded the ship. His boots glowed like oiled machinery. His robe had the pristine, unwrinkled look of clothing that had just been removed from a fabricator.

The vegetation in the room was as utilitarian as his robots. A standard vine species ran across the ceiling. Undistinguished trees occupied a few spots. The flower bed tucked into one of the corners had borders that could have been plotted with a laser.

He nodded toward the robots. "I should advise you: my serving machines are equipped with quick-acting immobilization moles. I don't want to sound rude, but I felt I should warn you. I'm linked to every machine on this ship by way of the Voice. They'll respond the moment I think the appropriate command."

He pointed at Ganmei. "The door behind me is the door to my private bedroom. Go in the bedroom and take off your clothes."

Ganmei stared at him. She started to step back, and the Voice of the ship boomed out of a loudspeaker.

"That was an order. Go in the bedroom. Take off your clothes."

Ganmei lowered her head. She stepped across the room with her hands clasped in front of her stomach, and a robot followed her through the door.

A screen lit up on my right. Ganmei was standing in front of a bed. She bent forward and pulled her shirt over her head.

Our captor watched her intently. "I presume you and she have been enjoying the customary pleasures."

I drew myself up. I had decided I should act nonchalant and try to keep him talking, but it was already beginning to take an effort.

"It depends on what you consider customary," I said.

"Is there anything she's particularly good at? Anything you would recommend I have her do?"

"I'm afraid that's not an area in which I can give you much information. My sexual proclivities tend to be singularly prosaic—except for a tendency to place a ridiculously high value on certain kinds of emotions."

"You've been with this one for several years now. Isn't that unusual for you?"

"Actually, we've really only had a few tendays together. The rest of the time I've been immersed in a secondary personality."

"And what exactly is your secret? How have you managed to befuddle so many women?"

I shrugged. "I'm afraid there have been a lot of them mostly because I can't seem to settle on one for very long."

"But I gather you don't seem to have any trouble manipulating them into giving you what you want."

"In practice, it doesn't normally require much manipulation."

"There's just something about you women find irresistible, is that it?"

"I try to give them a good time. I let them know how I feel about them. Most people like being the absolute center of someone else's life—at least for awhile."

"I'd rather *take* what I want," he said. "Isn't that the way it's supposed to be? The way human beings were *meant* to be?"

He slipped into one of his rants about genetically enhanced humans. Mankind didn't need the kind of biological divide they were creating, he proclaimed. Machines would always be superior to human brains.

"I've been working with machine intelligence since I was a child," he said. "There's no limit. Machine-assisted intelligence is the only future mankind can look forward to."

He had kept his eyes on the screen while he delivered his oration. His voice had risen as he reached the end, but he had gone on talking to me over his shoulder. Our model had indicated he was looking for anxiety and inner torment, and Ganmei was offering him a well-calculated display of both. She walked around restlessly. She sat on the edge of the bed with her head drooping. She stared at the door as if she was simultaneously afraid it would open and tired of waiting for it to open.

"Your companion seems restless," he said. "This must be a trying moment for a mind like hers. Isolated from her normal sources of intellectual stimulation. Forced to contemplate the trivial worries that preoccupy lesser intellects."

It was the most revealing thing he had said. Most of Ganmei's consciousness was probably absorbed in a couple of her intellectual preoccupations. She could have acted a complete scene from a classic drama while she was engaging in a detailed review of her plans for her telescope array. If he didn't know that, he didn't really understand the power of the cells packed in her skull.

You weren't aware she was thinking about other things when you were with her. You thought you were receiving all the attention a human personality could concentrate on you. Then she would say something that indicated another part of her brain had been developing a lengthy, complicated train of thought.

Once she had returned me to my baseline personality while she kept an eye on the robots that were constructing her second telescope. To me, she had been totally absorbed in all the things we had done. We had made love, we had talked, we had even played several games of Go for some reason. And there hadn't been a moment, in all that time, when she had stopped watching the information the construction robots were pouring into her communications implant. She had even made a number of minor corrections in their programs.

Our tormentor stood up. He tipped back his head and smiled as he looked me over. "Perhaps it's time I gave you both something to think about."

You didn't need a personality model to predict his next moves. He left the camera on after he entered the bedroom, so I would have to watch his depredations. He ordered Ganmei to kneel. He told her he wanted to see what she could do with her mouth.

You could see the surprise on his face when she swayed to her knees in front of him. He stared down at her as if he was hypnotized. Ganmei put her hands on one of his silly boots and began kneading the material.

I started to turn my head away. Then I realized her fingers were working their way upward—toward the bare thigh above his boot.

Ganmei grabbed his robe as soon as his face started to slacken. She put her shoulder under his chest and used him as a shield as she stood up. It was a nice move, but he had apparently transmitted an order before he lost consciousness. The robot rolled around the room faster than she could turn his body.

I had lunged at the robot next to me as soon as I had seen Red Boots react to Ganmei's anesthetic. My hands had reached for the arm that had been fitted with a projectile launcher. The robot fired at me at point-blank range, but I still managed to place my hands on each side of the arm and rub them up and down.

Ganmei's mole was an anesthetic. Her victim had slipped into unconsciousness. The moles the robots had fired at us were paralytics. I was still conscious, but my limbs were frozen. Naturally, Ganmei was the first to realize we were only paralyzed from the neck down. Her voice reached me over the loudspeaker seconds after the paralytic took effect.

She had developed some exceptionally powerful moles, so there was some hope we would recover before Red Boots did. "Open the bedroom door and attack the robot as soon as we're both free," Ganmei said. "It will probably paralyze you again, but I'll attack it while it's focused on you."

It was a reasonable idea, but the robot in the bedroom vetoed it before I could take a step toward the door. It paralyzed her as soon as it detected the first involuntary movement she made when the paralytic wore off. Then it started rolling toward the door.

Ganmei didn't hesitate. "Turn around and head for the other door, Joe. *Now*. It looks like Plan B will have to do."

The wheel was a series of adjoining rooms, just like the wheel on our ship. The other door in the throne room connected to a room that housed the elevator we had used when the robots had herded us between the hub and the wheel. There were no manual controls on the elevator. I would have to use the emergency hatch located in the ceiling in front of the elevator door.

I've always had trouble visualizing the actual situation in spinning space environments. I like to feel that down is *down*. I don't like to think I'm standing inside the rim of a slowly turning wheel, with my head pointed toward a hub that contains a nuclear reactor, three huge rocket nozzles, and all the other gadgetry and wiring that gives me some hope I will eventually reach a more comprehensible destination.

In this case, I pulled myself *up* to enter the escape hatch. My muscles still felt they were climbing as they carried me along the ladder, but something in my head rebelled against the idea that the hub was up. I crawled toward my objective with my body telling me one thing and my brain telling me something else.

The shaft made a sharp turn and merged with the shaft that contained the elevator. The ladder ran along the tracks the elevator used. I could look "down" and see the top of the elevator car.

If there's one thing I know something about, it's the art of escape and evasion. When you've lived the way I have, you acquire some experience with the stratagems of decamping. I stopped a few meters above the elevator car and rubbed my magic hands along one of the tracks. A section about the length of my forearm dissolved into dust, and I continued on my way.

The car came to life a few seconds later. It whirred up the track and stopped with a satisfying bump when it hit the break in the track. Then I looked down and realized I hadn't been as smart as I thought. I had forgotten about the hatch in the roof.

I slipped off the ladder and let the spin carry me down to the car. I examined it for a couple of sweaty minutes—Ganmei would have known what to do as soon as she looked at it—and applied my hands. I eliminated another section of the ladder for good measure, and continued on my way.

None of it would have worked if machines were as smart as Red Boots thought they were. A normal, unenhanced human would have realized I was trying to reach the hub and headed me off. Fortunately, our captor had given them an improvised message when he realized he was losing consciousness, and the Voice of the ship had decided the robots were supposed to "pursue" me. They didn't catch up to me until I had reached the control room, located the emergency communications system, and transmitted six encoded microsecond blips. Five of the blips were all-points pleas for help, with a description of our situation. The fourth blip in the series was a special message for two very special people.

"They'll know we're here," I said. "Every authority in the solar system will know what you've done to us. They can probably figure out exactly who you are."

Red Boots looked at me as if he thought I was a lunatic. "Do you seriously think someone is going to put together a rescue expedition and come out here on a ten-year round trip? Just to look for you? Or a forty-year trip if you attract rescuers who feel they have to conserve their resources and do the job on the cheap."

"Ganmei is a public figure. She has admirers all over the system."

"And they all know they could spend decades looking for you after they invested all that time coming here. It seems to me you went to a lot of trouble just to send a useless message. You may be intelligent, Ganmei, but you obviously aren't very creative."

"We thought we could get you under control," Ganmei said. "Obviously it was a foolish idea."

She had been propped against a wall of the bedroom, still naked and paralyzed. His robots had hit her with a third dose of the paralytic when she had recovered from the second dose a few minutes after he regained consciousness.

"Your little friend may feel it was especially foolish. I've been moving your ship close to a small ice object. My machines have already started transferring reaction mass to your tanks. In approximately twelve hours, I'm going to return him to your ship and propel him to the outer edge of the belt, where he'll take up a long, slow orbit around the sun."

"That's murder," Ganmei said. "He'll die if you leave him out there, cut off from medical treatment."

"For you, I'm preparing a very pleasant boudoir. Our relationship may be a little unusual, since it seems I can't touch you without incurring some risk. But I presume I and my ship will eventually develop some kind of counter mole."

"There are even things you can do before then," I said. "I've been in two or three similar situations myself."

On the screen, I could see Ganmei start. She lowered her head and stared at the floor.

Red Boots frowned at me. "I thought you only performed for willing partners."

I gave him an airy wave of my hand. "There have been times when I was physically cut off from the person who had captured my fancy. There was a time when I was in my fifties—a period when I seem to have been especially inclined to engage in sentimentality—when I fell in love with a woman who had been confined to a completely sterile environment. She was a biodesigner. One of her mistakes had done some strange things to her immune system. I thought I was merely offering her a little long-distance companionship when I first contacted her. Then I discovered my feelings were more erotic than I had realized."

"And you actually engaged in some form of sexual activity?"

"It was much more satisfying than you would think. For human beings, *talk* is a very important aspect of sexual pleasure. Talk and feeling. If you can talk—and you have the right feelings—all kinds of acts can seem quite soul stirring."

I had blurted out my first story on an impulse, but I had been almost certain it would capture his attention. It wasn't the first time I've met a man who wanted to hear everything I could tell him. Usually I don't spend a lot of time recounting my romantic adventures. For one thing, I tend to become engrossed in the next one as soon as the last one ends. But we all feel the need to spend a little time talking about the part of our life that is special and important. Soldiers talk about war. Musicians chatter about music.

He knew I was trying to extend my stay, of course. He started calling me Scheherazade.

"Tell me another story, Sherry. See how long you can delay the inevitable—the moment when I send you to a place where your memories will be your only consolation. Or did you bring a few shadows to help you entertain yourself when your hyper-intelligent paramour was engrossed in her engineering project?"

I used up both of my sex-at-a-distance experiences by the end of the first day cycle. When I went to bed that night, the Voice of the ship reminded me I could be awakened at any time and returned to Ganmei's ship. The next morning, when he invited me to breakfast, I told him my romance with a famous ballerina had been more eccentric than the information in the databanks indicated.

"She used to dance for me when we were alone," I lied. "That was all she would ever do."

"And you just sat there and watched her, Sherry?"

"She had me choose her costumes. I picked her costumes and I choreographed her dances from a list of ballet movements she gave me. She said she had a problem with actual physical contact."

"But she wanted to place herself under your control? She had broken through her superficial social conditioning and yielded to her female need to be controlled?"

"I suppose you could look at it that way."

His eyes moistened. "How about nudity? Did your choice of costumes include nudity?"

"Of course."

As I had hoped, he decided that would be just the kind of thing he should do with Ganmei. This time, he turned off the camera when he disappeared into the bedroom.

I stood by the big chair—it was the only chair in the room—and retreated into imaginary conversations with Ganmei. The real torment in this situation was my inability to communicate with her. I could assume she understood what I was doing. But did she approve? Did she understand I didn't normally think about those kinds of fantasies? Would she feel she had exposed a different side of my personality?

"I couldn't have handled this without you," Ganmei had told me several times. "I probably would have been completely baffled by his personality structure. I can build the models. I can understand the theory. But I can't really understand what he's feeling. I feel like

I'm trying to understand someone who belongs to a different species."

"That's just a matter of experience," I had argued. "You've been absorbed in technological and scientific matters all your life."

"Can you understand it? Can you actually relate his feelings to anything *you* feel?"

"I've met a lot of people in the last hundred and thirty years. I've never felt any great need to control other people myself. I'm basically a pleasure-oriented person, and that's all I ever will be. But I've known plenty of people who obviously have to spend their lives making other people do things. Human sexuality—especially male sexuality—is a complicated business. It can get mixed up with a lot of other things."

"I don't think I'll understand it if I live a whole millennium," Ganmei had insisted. "Not emotionally. It just seems so *stupid*."

I had wrestled with a surge of irrational emotion when we passed the tenth hour. I had promised myself I wouldn't start worrying until we had waited at least thirty hours for an answer.

The dancing fantasy kept Red Boots occupied for most of the morning. He ate lunch sitting in his big chair while I stood a few steps to one side.

"Tell me another story, Sherry. Add to my stock of wisdom."

I could have felt some sympathy for him under other circumstances. He had obviously developed one of the three alternate personality structures predicted by our model (and by ordinary, reasonably well-informed observation of human behavior). He couldn't approach a woman unless he believed he was in absolute control of the situation.

He had verified most of the assumptions in our model when he had selected an immobilizer that paralyzed its victims from the neck down. Ganmei had been absolutely powerless when she had been paralyzed, but she had still been conscious, and he could still make her respond.

A competent personality modification technician could have given him a new life in a single tenday. Ganmei's assessment had been right on target. Strengthen the chemistry of assertiveness, remove the accidental conditioning that made him feel women would reject him—and you would have a human male with a totally intact ability to approach a human female and suggest they have dinner together. Instead, he had clung to the damaged personality structure he had acquired from the haphazard interplay of his genes and his childhood environment.

He lolled on his chair. He gorged on the fruits and pastries arranged on a serving cart. He nodded knowingly when I reached critical points in my narratives. He reminded me that my ultimate destiny was a womanless isolation.

"Work, Sherry. Make it good. Hold off the inevitable for another hour."

But he did listen. He was one of the easiest audiences I could have asked for. I had thrown out a few probes when I started my story telling, to see how much he knew. After that, I knew he would accept any erotic detail I offered him. How would he know it couldn't be true? There are things you can't learn from shadows.

You could have summed up the essence of his personality structure with one sentence: he was trying to turn a real woman into a pixel shadow. Real women have desires and needs of their own. Shadows have the needs and desires you give them.

Ganmei knew that, too, and she seemed to be giving him what he wanted. His third session in the bedroom lasted almost six hours. He dropped into his chair when he came out and folded his hands over his stomach as if he had just eaten a particularly satisfying meal.

"Your advice has been very helpful, Sherry. Very helpful. I probably should have left the camera on—so you'd know exactly what we're going to be doing while you putter around in your empty ship for the next forty or fifty years. Perhaps you can console yourself by writing your memoirs. Like that legendary character they keep comparing you to."

I let him see my anguish. It gave him another incentive to keep me around.

If I were creating a video drama, I would drag out the suspense and pretend our salvation arrived just as I was being escorted to the airlock for my final transfer to Ganmei's ship. The truth was more mundane. The loudspeakers started booming while Red Boots and Ganmei were once again isolated in the bedroom. And I was standing beside the big chair planning my next set of lies.

"This is Sori, Joe. Your package has arrived. The password is the name of the composer who wrote the piece you were playing when you fell in love with the red-haired oboist in Hartford, Connecticut. Say the unforgettable name and it's all yours."

It had been thirty years since I had seen Sori. He had still been a tall, gangling twenty-plus, with a brain that never stopped churning and hormones that made him intensely aware he was surrounded by healthy women who had been interacting with men for more years than he had been alive. His voice sounded firmer and less bumptious, but I could still hear his pleasure in the effect he knew it would create. If I understood the meaning of that final "It's all yours," he had sent me something better than a virus. The password would activate a program that would give me control of the ship.

Unfortunately, he had taken my romantic proclamations at face value. I knew what he was talking about when he referred to the red-haired oboist. I had told him about her when I had been chattering about my own youthful emotions. I'll never forget the name of the composer who wrote the piece we were playing when I fell in love with her, I had said. He was an obscure Baroque musicsmith, but I'll never forget his name.

I could remember saying that. I could remember my exact words. The one thing I couldn't remember was the composer's name.

It had been thirty years since I had mentioned him to Sori. It had been a *hundred years* since the incident itself. I couldn't even remember the *oboist's* name.

I've never kept count of my love affairs. I'm not a collector. But when you've been pursuing the same passion for a hundred and thirty years… I'm afraid it does add up.

Hundreds of composers wrote sonatas and concertos between 1600 and 1750. Baroque enthusiasts had started mining the manuscript collections near the beginning of the 20th Century, and they had kept it up all through the 21st. Every musician I had ever played with had doted on pieces no one else had ever heard of. I had even run into a harpsichordist who was relentlessly assembling ensembles so she could eventually say she had played the harpsichord part in every one of the fifteen hundred cantatas Allesandro Scarlatti composed.

I couldn't think as fast as Ganmei and Red Boots, but years of experience had honed my fight or flight (mostly flight) reflexes. I'm happy to report that I had ducked behind the big chair while I had still been recognizing the problem Sori had unwittingly presented me. Boots had given his robots permanent orders after my last adventure had revealed the tricks I could play with my hands. They were supposed to stay at least six steps away from me.

It was a big gap when you didn't have a missile weapon of your own, but I had a small psychological advantage: I had been expecting a message. Boots, on the other hand, had been distracted by the activities taking place in the bedroom. He responded a lot faster than I would have, but I still had time to push the chair across the room and smash it into the robot before it could obey Boots' order and move into position for a shot. I slammed the robot into the wall and lunged for the door.

My communications implant belled as I reached the door. *What's the matter?* Ganmei asked. *Why haven't you given it the password?*

I can't remember the name. Sori has made a terrible mistake.

What are you doing? We have a standoff in here. I can't get near him. The robot has me covered.

I just pushed this robot against the wall with the chair. I'm going out the other door.

Can you block that door with the chair? Can you grab the bedroom door and hold it shut? Do it.

It was a moment when the conciseness of CM made all the difference. The blipped transmissions had bounced between us in seconds. I didn't know what she had in mind, but I decided I should give her superior brainpower the benefit of the doubt. I shoved the chair against the door and leaped across the room toward the bedroom.

Can you remember what kind of piece you played? Concerto grossi? Trio sonata? Concerto?

My hands seized the handle that secured the bedroom door. The door I had just barricaded with the chair opened inward, toward me. The door to the bedroom opened away from me, toward the bedroom.

I think it was a trio sonata. Why?

Stand by.

I clutched the door handle and positioned myself along the wall, so I could pull up on the handle and keep the door closed. Boots threw his weight on the handle on the other side of the door, and I leaned back and held on. He might be a lunatic, but he had equipped his doors with hefty, oversized no-nonsense space ship door handles. I could grip the handle with both hands. The door handles on space ships are always built large, with total disregard to aesthetics, for the same reason most of the doors are manually operated. You don't trust your life to slippery doorknobs and electronic circuits that might fail at awkward moments.

My first impression of him had been correct. He had been lolling around with his computer when he should have been exercising. He might think I was just a sexual convenience, but he was learning I had more primitive masculine virtues.

Scan this list. Say delete if you feel a name is well known.

"Release the door, Sherry. Release the door or your over-brained female friend will find out what it's like to be really helpless."

Names skimmed across my consciousness. Arne... Buxtehude... Cima... The CM word for delete is short and sharp but the names were rushing by at a tempo that made me feel like I was trying to follow a runaway metronome. Ganmei had over-estimated my processing speed. I eliminated Arne and Buxtehude but Geminiani, Pepusch, and a dozen others slipped past me. The list contained at least ninety names. She had left off the obvious composers like Bach and Purcell, but serious Baroque enthusiasts would have recognized half the list.

A noise behind me made me turn my head. Something was hitting the other door.

Your deletions have been executed. The list has been returned for further analysis.

I didn't know where Ganmei had obtained the list—or what she hoped to do with it. None of the unfamiliar names had jogged my memory. How could they? I was holding onto a door with a madman on the other side and the madman's robot assistants obviously gathering behind the other door.

My tug of war opponent tried a surprise release followed by a quick jerk. My body slipped along the wall, but I managed to recover before he could force me off balance.

"I'm not going to tell you again, Sherry. Ganmei has just been immobilized. I can approach her without the slightest concern for my safety. I realize I can't overcome her pain control system with the equipment I have here in the bedroom. But there is no limit to the physical damage I can inflict."

Ignore him. Hold the door.

I glanced at the other door and flinched when I saw the chair move. It was a small shift—just enough to be noticeable—but even the genetically obsolete organ inside my skull could foresee the inevitable consequences.

I had been resisting the impulse to send transmissions that would interrupt what Ganmei was doing—whatever it was she was doing. But I had to make sure she understood the situation.

The robots are beginning to move the other door. They don't have to open it all the way—they can create a small crack and slip a projectile arm through it.

"We know you're transmitting, Sherry. We'll be reading everything you say in minutes. In spite of that exotic language you're using."

He always said *we* when he referred to himself and the ship's computer system. He already saw himself as a component in a composite personality.

Listen carefully. I'm going to give you three names. When you have them—push the door inward. Rush into the bedroom. His Voice has probably shut off the microphones in the room you're in. Rush in and try the names. If you get control—tell the system to obey me, too. Get him immobilized. Don't let him set up a hostage situation. Here are the names—Paganelli. Pampani. Bartiomei.

The big chair scraped against the floor. I could see the other door edging open.

I hadn't even thought about the possibility the computer system could have turned off the mikes in the throne room. How long had it been since I had received Sori's message? Three minutes? Four? I had been shoved into a world in which everything seemed to be moving at megaspeeds. Ganmei had somehow come up with a list of composers and subjected it to some kind of analysis. And now I was supposed to blindly follow her instructions. In the same way I blindly trusted the decisions of computer programs when they manipulated my investments or guided the vehicles that carried me across years of vacuum.

I let go of the handle and pushed the door forward. I can even boast that I managed to do it with my eyes open. *Paganelli* isn't the most bloodthirsty war cry anyone ever uttered, but it was backed up with a scream that should have unnerved a battalion of Mongols. Boots fell back as the door flew open. I saw his knees bend and tried to catch him in a bear hug.

Frontal attacks aren't my normal style—in love or war. The self-defense maneuvers I've acquired are all variations on techniques used in aikido—a martial art in which you turn your opponent's motion against him. In this case, however, I thought I would be better off if I tangled us together and presented the robot with a confusing target while I babbled the names Ganmei had picked.

His reaction time wasn't as fast as Ganmei's but it was good enough. He recovered his balance and skipped away from me before I had covered half the distance between us. He broke into the beginnings of a smile—the same patronizing smile he had bestowed on me when he listened to my stories.

I twisted toward him, bellowing the names of the other two composers. I could see the robot in the corner on my left. On my right, Ganmei was lying on the floor, with a flimsy white gown spread around her. Her useless arms and legs were sprawled at random angles. She had to lift her head off the floor to see what we were doing.

I screamed an alternate pronunciation of Paganelli, and followed it with a squeaking, hysterical Pampani that emphasized the second syllable. Ganmei had accented the first syllable but that didn't mean Sori—or the computer system—had settled on the same choice. Most of the musicians I had played with seemed to pronounce the names of the less familiar composers according to their whims. I had been playing Baroque music for one hundred years, and I still couldn't give you a definitive answer if you asked me if the name of England's most famous Baroque composer was pronounced *Pur*cell or Pur*cell*. I'd never met anyone else who could, either.

"Welcome, Joe," the loudspeaker said. "Please stand by while the installation procedure proceeds."

Don't try to grab him, Ganmei transmitted. *Stay between him and me.*

Ganmei could think faster than Red Boots, but she was firing orders at a body that still retained the reaction time it had been issued when it was conceived in the last decade of the 20th Century. I managed to stop myself in midmotion but I stumbled when I tried to change course. I flopped down to one knee and scrambled to my feet with my arms flailing for balance.

Boots could have run straight at Ganmei while I had been fumbling. Instead, he had come to a sudden stop. His jaw had gone slack. He was staring at the air as if he was looking at a vision.

He's lost contact with the ship. He's disoriented.

The disorientation only lasted a few seconds—just long enough for me to edge sideways and place myself between him and Ganmei. Even without his computer link, he was still smarter and faster than the baseline human standing between him and a defenseless female body.

His face changed again. All his bland, round-faced composure vanished as if he had rubbed it off with a towel. His face twisted into the most unnerving mask I've ever seen on a human head.

Just stay between us. That's all you have to do. He isn't armed, but he can still make serious threats if he gets into position. That's his best bet at this point.

For the first time since we had come aboard, I was staring at the rage that had driven him all the way to the Kuiper Belt just so he could torment a human female. Ganmei didn't have to describe the things he could threaten. The creature poised in front of me could have shattered her skull with his feet. And tramped the fragments into the floor.

His mouth was wide open when he charged, but he came at me with complete, unnerving silence. I dropped to one knee just before he hit, and applied one of my self-defense techniques to his robe. I knew I was disobeying Ganmei—I was sending him *past* her, just a step from one of her feet. But I couldn't believe I could grapple with the emotional energies that had created that face.

He stumbled away from me, but his reflexes were still functioning. He recovered before he hit the wall and started to turn. I slammed into him from the side and held on as if I was clinging to a lifeline. Teeth sank into my cheek. Knees jabbed at my groin. Hands pulled at my ears.

"Welcome, Joseph Louis Baske. This ship is now under your command. Your voice characteristics have been analyzed and recorded. You may issue your directions in any of the six accepted international languages."

"*Immobilize the man in the red boots! Have the robots fire paralyzer projectiles at the man in the red boots. Do it!*"

He was screaming into my ear when his body started to slacken. He was still screaming five minutes after the moles took effect.

Ganmei hadn't told me, but she had loaded every Baroque-related entry in the latest *Grove's* into her auxiliary memory before we had left the asteroid belt. There had been a number of occasions during our voyage when I had been impressed by her knowledge of Baroque music. I hadn't realized she had been running high-speed searches while we conversed.

"I knew it was one of your major interests," she said. "I thought our conversations would work out better if I didn't have to keep asking you to explain things."

The whole brouhaha had lasted approximately five minutes, counting from the moment we had first heard Sori's announcement. In that time, she had pulled out all the composer's names in her Baroque files, eliminated the ones she immediately recognized, sent me the list of seventy, and reduced the remainder to eight names by applying half a dozen sieves based on her knowledge of my taste and attitudes. Then she had read the complete entries for all eight composers and reduced the list to three.

She had remained formidably rational under the worst possible pressure. He had terrorized Ganmei more than I had realized. He had kept her paralyzed for most of the time she had been imprisoned in his bedroom. He had stood over her, while she lay there helpless, and described all the things he could do to her. I wasn't the only person who had realized he could kick her to death. She had almost blacked out, she said, when I let him go past me.

"My entire body turned into one big fear response," Ganmei said. "You did the right thing when you ignored my instructions. I can see that now. But then—there was nothing between him and me."

Overall, I thought we had both done well. I had made some major contributions, but I had let her take control when that was obviously the best thing to do. We worked like a well-coordinated team when we disposed of our prisoner, too. We both agreed we had to contact the proper authorities and obtain permission for a temporary involuntary personality modification. The authorities concurred, and we administered the modification program and launched him on a forty-year voyage to the inner solar system. We would have put him on a five-year trajectory, but our governmental overseers vetoed the idea. They didn't think we should send a giant iceball careening toward civilization with a former lunatic an elevator ride from the control room.

I slipped into my secondary personality after two tendays of luxurious dinners, pleasant physical contact, and a general atmosphere of good-natured harmony. And the next time I returned to my baseline personality, I discovered I had spent twenty tendays—over half an Earth year!—pursuing my musical mania.

I had known the time was passing, of course. It just hadn't mattered to me. I had regained my normal personality because the secondary included a component that shut it down when its preoccupation reached absurd lengths.

Ganmei was working in her laboratory when I located her.

"Have we got another problem, Ganmei?"

"I couldn't help it, Joe. I just kept putting it off."

"It's been over *half an Earth year.*"

"It isn't you."

"Then what is it?"

"It's what he did to me. I tried to keep my feelings under control. It wouldn't have been fair to you if I hadn't. But after you resumed your secondary. And I went back to work—"

"The last time I held you I felt like all the things that separate us had been temporarily dissolved. That was just a performance? You're telling me you kept your real emotions hidden after we got him under control?"

"*I can't help it, Joe.* I've never been through anything like that. And don't tell me we can order a therapy program. The therapies are all deconditioning procedures. You apply the procedure and remove a bad association."

"It's a standard procedure for people who've been raped and assaulted. I've even been told it can be rather pleasant—that the programs overwhelm the bad association by strengthening good associations."

"I'm not talking about an irrational association. I learned something. I learned what people are like. What they're capable of. I thought I knew."

"He was an aberration. You saw the model. He's just a silly accident. An error. He doesn't tell us anything about human nature."

"An aberration created by the strength of the human sex drive—a drive we don't even need anymore. Deconditioning programs aren't the only way to deal with it."

I stared at her. "It would be a mistake. I've thought about doing that myself a few times. Eliminate your sexual feelings and you eliminate emotions that lie at the root of all kinds of other feelings. Warmth. Tenderness. Joie de vivre."

"And cruelty. And subjugation."

I stepped toward her and saw her stiffen in response. "You can't spend all these years alone, Ganmei. No human being can do that. You understood that when I first approached you."

"That's not what I'm talking about. You know that's not what I'm talking about."

I stretched my arms in front of me. "That's as close as I'll come to you if that's how you feel. I'll stay on the other side of the room if you want me to. But I'm not going to spend the next twelve years hiding in that artificial personality."

"And what will you be thinking while you're carefully staying out of reach? Won't you really be thinking this is just a temporary situation? And sooner or later I'll realize you aren't like him?"

I stepped back, deliberately widening the distance between us. "Do you think I came here, all this way, just so I can experience some commonplace physical sensation? I can always get that from shadows if I have to. I came here to *connect* with you, Ganmei. To make contact. In all the ways two people can touch each other. We've been throwing lifelines across the biggest gulf that ever separated a man and a woman. Bigger than wealth or class. Bigger than religion or clan loyalty or all the other barriers societies have interposed between men and women. Do you think I can't live with another gulf, too, if that's necessary?"

I meant it, too. And she knew I meant it. I was summarizing the attitude that's guided my whole life. Anyone who had spent an hour looking at the databanks would know I meant it.

They would also know, of course, that she was right, and I would be waiting for the moment when I could step across that gulf and add a dab of physical contact to our relationship. Ganmei might be more intelligent than me, but she was a woman, too. Her words were telling me I was confronted with a fortress, but her eyes and the tone of her voice were advising me I was looking at an emotional battleground.

It took almost a year. I held her against me three hundred and forty-eight days after I had taken my vow of non-contact—and the fact that I know the exact count should tell you all you need to know about my feelings. We were talking about the wine we had just drunk when she suddenly lowered her head and took two hesitant steps in my direction. And I gathered up my nerve and took the final step for her.

But that was in the future. In the meantime, the obsolete human and the future human had to start reconstructing the relationship they had been fashioning before the aberrant human interrupted them.

We began—how else?—by playing Bach together.

AFTERWORD: GIACOMO CASANOVA

Giacomo Casanova was born in Venice in 1725 and died in a central European castle in 1798. His travels took him the length and breadth of Europe—from London to Moscow, from Holland to Constantinople. His active years spanned the decades when 18th Century European society was at its height and he got a good look at the whole show. He fought duels, talked to famous people like Voltaire and Frederick the Great, engineered a famous prison escape, swindled aristocrats with scams based on numerology and astrology, tried his hand at careers in soldiering and the priesthood, and became wealthy operating a franchise of a French government lottery. He even played the violin in an opera house during a period when he was temporarily down and out.

He didn't become a legend, however, because of his conversations with celebrities and his prowess as a tourist. Casanova's memoirs cover almost 4,000 printed pages in the standard English translation Willard Trask published in the 1960s. Most of the words on those pages depict Casanova's love affairs. He conducted over 120 love affairs during the period described in the memoirs—and he died before he could finish chronicling his amours.

Other men have written memoirs that included their sexual adventures, but they are usually figures, like H.G. Wells, who are famous for other reasons. Casanova's love affairs were the central activity of his life. Each section of his memoirs, with very few exceptions, is the story of a love affair. The other items—the duels, his travels—are brought up almost in passing.

"Feeling that I was born for the sex opposite to mine," Casanova says in his foreword, "I have always loved it and done everything I could to make myself loved by it." Later, he divides his life into three phases. In the first phase, he says, he attracted women by his person. In the second, his person had lost some of its appeal, but he had acquired wealth. In the third, he had neither wealth nor person, and he had to do the best he could.

He was definitely not the kind of man who simply grabs any woman who happens to be available. He pursued particular women who had aroused his interest, one woman at a time, and the women who captivated him were never merely sources of physical pleasure. He always gives you some sense of their personalities. Seventy-five percent of carnal pleasure, he says, is *talk*.

In the middle of the 20th Century, a fifteen-year-old would-be writer encountered Casanova in a book called *Twelve Against the Gods, the Story of Adventure* by a writer named William Bolitho. Bolitho argued that Casanova was a successful lover because he fell in love with every woman he pursued. Time after time, Bolitho pointed out, we see Casanova squandering huge sums and taking enormous risks just so he can win the favor of the woman who has become his current obsession.

To Casanova, Bolitho wrote, "A sweetheart was not a postprandial dish nor any of the other things a pseudo-libertine makes of her: a trophy, a prey, or an instrument. His love for any of them was as real as any that led to holy matrimony; only it did not last." Casanova attracted women, Bolitho argued, because he gave them "all that he had, all that he was" in a "lump sum" instead of doling it out "in a lifetime of installments."

Bolitho's portrait of Casanova presented a picture that appealed to the young would-be writer's teenage mind. There are other ways to view Casanova, but the memoirs certainly make a good case for Bolitho's suggestion that he was a serial monogamist. Tom read the (very) condensed version of Casanova's memoirs that the Modern Library published in a slim volume, and felt it didn't contradict Bolitho's portrait. Later, he read an illustrated biography of Casanova by the British novelist John Masters, and the third volume of the Trask translation of the memoirs. Eventually, he read all six volumes. Over the years, in addition, Tom encountered Casanova in books on special subjects such as Baroque music. The memoirs are considered a primary source for information about life in 18th Century Europe.

In his mid-50s, Tom returned to writing stories for the science fiction magazines and inserted a character based on Casanova into a short story. The Viennese adventurer still appealed to Tom's romantic instincts, even though he was a thoroughly monogamous husband who had shared over thirty years of his life with a supremely satisfactory wife. For some people, the ultimate romantic act is a lifelong commitment. For others, romance involves less lasting relationships. It occurred to Tom that a character based on Casanova could travel through a future interplanetary society in the same way the real Casanova had traversed 18th Century Europe. He could start his odyssey on the Moon, then move on to other worlds. Tom sat down at his computer....